THE MEANDER TILE OF
LISA
GRECO

A ROMANCE OF MYTHIC IDENTITY

ANDREA AGUILLARD

LOS ANGELES
2017

STORY MERCHANT BOOKS

The Meander Tile of Lisa Greco

ISBN 10: 0-9981628-9-2

ISBN 13: 978-09981628-9-8

Story Merchant Books
400 S. Burnside Avenue #11B
Los Angeles, CA 90036
www.storymerchantbooks.com

Interior Design: Danielle Canfield, www.529Books.com

Cover Design: Dafeenah Jamal, www.IndieDesignz.com

ALSO BY ANDREA AGUILLARD:

The Twaesum Aik of Brae Mackenzie

Coming Soon:

The Circling Stones of Allison Reid

We are like the spider.
We weave our life and then move along in it.
We are like the dreamer who dreams and then lives in the dream.
This is true for the entire universe.

—Upanishads

For Andrea McKeown
My lifelong inspiration

THE MEANDER TILE OF
LISA
GRECO

One

YOU CAN BE SO WOUND up in your daily grind that destiny can slip by behind your back. Ever since Lisa Greco stumbled onto the Yale Publishing Course, then got hired at graduation by Standard House, she'd learned to work her head off, and pretend her personal dreams never existed. Awakening early every morning, she ran, rain or shine, sleet or snow, the 3.35-mile loop around Prospect Park. Then she donned her knightly business-suit armor—colors ranging from gray to black to gray—and grabbed a Q train into Manhattan. She worked feverishly on other people's novels, other people's stories, and other people's charts and reports. And because that work danced close enough around her deepest desires, she lost herself in it.

She'd gotten damned good at it.

How good, she learned one winter morning when she staggered into her pod of an office on time despite the bloody blizzard, to discover that her beloved boss of ten years was lying in wait for her with a look on his face she couldn't decipher.

Kevin Boyle grabbed her elbow and steered her into his office—a real one, in the corner. "I've got bad news, and good news."

Her eyebrows rose in question as she handed him his decaf latte she'd not forgotten despite the extra, freezing, block it meant.

"I've submitted my resignation." He opened the steaming hot coffee with an appreciative smile. "It's time to go a-wanderin'. I'm afraid you're about to lose your arch-supporter, cheerleader, and champion here in this incubator of libraries."

"That is bad news, although you wandering anywhere sounds enviable. I'm the one who longs to wander." Lisa was stunned, as if the magic carpet were being pulled out from under her. Her career, begotten from financial necessity and from the practicality breathed into her by the Buffalo family she'd escaped from, was instantly revealed for what it was—a big fat compromise. She was about to comment further, when Kevin continued.

"I'm guessing you're wondering if there's good news. Management, who unofficially welcome my departure since my salary was already a thorn in their side, has already chosen my successor."

Her face went white, as the blood drained from it—her usual fight or flight response to danger.

"Don't you want to know who it is?"

"I'm afraid to ask," she finally managed to respond. Kevin looked like he'd just swallowed a triple chocolate bonbon.

"It's you."

Her eyes widened. She stared at him like a fawn caught in headlamps. "That's not funny," she said.

"It took them about sixty seconds to decide. They certainly weren't going to offer exec editor to someone who'd cost about as much as I do. Which means they had to fill it from inside the ranks."

"Which left them with only, what, a dozen other choices?"

"As I said," Kevin went on smoothly, with that genial look on his face that made her adore him despite the impossible authors he loaded onto her chock-full work schedule. "Actually, it took them less than sixty seconds. Clearly I trained you well. And I have to say I played it just right. I didn't even recommend you. I just looked them in the eye and shrugged my shoulders. Which, by the way, they probably didn't notice because they were off to the next marketing meeting."

Lisa was speechless. What was he saying? "What now?" she asked.

"You're scheduled to meet with Phyllis at ten tomorrow morning, to hear the salary they have in mind."

"You don't know?"

He chuckled. "They made it clear it was none of my business anymore. You know how our beloved new corporate zeitgeist hangs," he added. "Seamless compartmentalization. The one percent don't consult downward anymore."

Kevin's phone rang, and he gave her his "excuse-me" eyes. As she stood and walked out, she took a closer look at his office. In all these years she'd barely allowed herself to notice the details—it was just plain too far above her pay level. His was a *corner* office for chrissakes, on the forty-fourth floor, with a drop-dead view of lower Manhattan and across the Hudson all the way to the Jersey shore. Its furniture was real: real oak desk, real leather-padded executive chair. A battery of phones. And, most of all, a door that closed and locked. It had walls. Which meant privacy—something she had not one minute's shot at in her five years at the company. She shuddered with a twinge of claustrophobia.

Lisa moved through the day in a daze, avoiding everyone who didn't literally bump into her. She went through the motions of proofing jacket copy, arguing cover design, writing a memo to marketing to get them excited about a new book, and signing rejection letters delivered by the pool secretary who never bothered to look at her.

Then, it was finally over—the place quieting as it emptied out. When she looked up from her computer it was six-fifteen. Past time to bail. She shuffled together the evening's reading and took a deep breath of relief when the elevator opened empty.

It wasn't until she grabbed the last available seat on the jam-packed B Train that it hit her. Like a slap in the face.

An iron fist in her gut.

By the time the train screeched into the Grand Army Plaza station in Park Slope the mood had settled down to the depths of her consciousness like a soggy quilt dropped from two stories up in August.

This turn of events definitely merited a priority stop at Sammie's, where she made a zombie bee-line for the end seat at the bar. Thank God Sammie Goldman, the owner-bartender, was too busy jumping to fill after-work drinks to initiate his evening interrogation. His eyebrows simply went up as she sat, and her eyes confirmed what he was asking: "the usual."

Two minutes later, the extra cold Metropolitan sat in front of her, delivered with a heartfelt grunt.

She grunted back as she lifted it to toast him, and took her first sip.

What the hell could possibly be bugging her? An editor's fondest dream come true. Why wasn't she dancing on the bar instead of moping in the corner?

Executive Editor Kevin Boyle's twenty-year-gig, prestigious as it was, was also indeed one helluva lot more work. Forget about weekends to yourself, the concept she still paid lip service to even though she'd never much experienced it. Forget about extra vacation days at her friend Cesca's posh manor in the Hamptons. Forget about turning off the phone to ensure a good night's sleep. She knew what Kevin's phone life was like.

And she knew very well she could handle it, no matter how much harder she'd have to work. Who knows where it might lead next? If Kevin had been younger when he made executive editor—as young as she was now, for example—he would have ended up publisher long ago. Everyone loved him. Every single woman over thirty-five gave him "right of first refusal" when she needed a man at her side for an author's or publisher's party, or celebratory dinner at Michael's, or even a weekend getaway to the Poconos. His dance card was like the Social Registry Blue Book. Images flashed in front of her eyes, of Jesus on the mountaintop being tempted by Satan. But what did Satan have to do with a job offer that would set all forty or so editors of her generation drooling with envy?

Was her Catholic background the problem? Was she feeling *guilty,* for chrissakes? Unworthy? Selfish?

She lifted her almost-empty glass, and Sammie gave an eye-nod of acknowledgement and reached for his shaker. She was in the middle of her first sip from the second icy-cold Metropolitan when it struck her. Another goddam line from the goddam Bible:

> When I was a child, I thought as a child.
>
> I spoke as a child...
>
> Now that I am a—

—woman, she mentally edited—

> I think as a woman, I speak as a woman,
>
> I act as a woman. And I must put away
>
> The things of a child.

Well, she thought, taking another sip of the drink and appreciating it, I'm certainly *drinking* like a woman.

A flood of thoughts inundated her inner chatroom, which, instead of being hushed by the alcohol, was only stimulated to garrulity. She'd noticed some time ago that she ordered a *second* drink only when she felt that something was troubling her, but had no idea, yet, what it was. Her days were so filled with a million details one on top of the other that her mind was forced to spin, laser-like, from one challenge to the next. It sometimes took major decompressing for the one negative thing that was bothering her to bubble up to a level of consciousness where it could be analyzed and confronted. Ritual alcohol was an excellent time-management tool. Instead of allowing her brooding the two or three days of dark moods it might take before arriving at the reason, Lisa could accomplish it in three drinks or under. Such was the rationalization that led her to raise her glass again.

But Sammie Goldman was deep in conversation with a tall, thin, and dapper older man whose stylish green jacket and yellow trousers perfectly accentuated the elegance of his demeanor so he took a few seconds longer than usual to see the glint of Lisa's quickly draining glass. Catching his acknowledging wink, she sipped the last drop and set it down carefully.

After shaking the cocktail, Sammie looked at her again, then said something to the man. At the same moment, the seat beside her emptied.

Dapper Man appeared at her side, bearing her third libation. Despite her mounting discomfort, she couldn't help noticing with approval that he carried the Metropolitan by the stem—to avoid warming it with a hand on the bowl of the glass.

"Signorina," the tall man said, with a throaty accent she immediately identified as southern Italian because it reminded her of her grandfather's. "My friend the bartender," he nodded toward Sammie, who gave her another wink, "suggested you might like some-one to talk to, and regrets that he's unable at the moment to play that role himself."

Without asking her permission, he settled gracefully on the available stool.

Rather than reacting with annoyance, as she well might have done all things being equal, she felt a wave of comfort and safety settle over her as though her Guardian Angel had materialized at her side. At a bar. Yup, I'm losing it. She raised her glass to toast the messenger who'd brought it. "Thank you," she said, when she set the glass down. "Very kind." She'd definitely take this one slowly.

Minutes passed. Dapper Man sipped his red wine, as if to say, I'm just fine if you don't have to say anything at all.

She appreciated the gallant gesture but, after all, she was a pro-fessional communicator. Silence, though much appreciated, was not her forte. "Do I look desperate or something?" she asked.

The man turned his dark eyes to appraise her face. She noticed that, though old enough to be her grandfather, he was quite attrac-tive. He took his time studying her, and she could feel the simple honesty of his judgement. "Let's just say you look deeply uncertain."

Her outburst of laughter broke through any ice that might have formed between them. She flashed back to the moment in a Blessed Trinity confessional in fourth grade when a priest about the same age as this man had laughed out loud at her reported sin: "I had nasty thoughts about my mother at least 100 times." "Only 100?" the priest had asked. Which made her laugh too. She felt like a loser when she walked out of the confessional with a Penance of one "Hail Mary." Her classmates saw her face redden, but she'd thought better of telling them why. Let their imaginations run wild.

"You look tense," the man said, "much more tense than an attractive young woman need ever be."

"I just got offered my boss's job," she replied, as though that explained anything.

He waited, without wrinkling his solemn attentiveness.

"It's one of the top management jobs in my company," she added, by way of illuminating her mood. "Probably with twice the pay I get now."

He nodded. "Congratulations. Why aren't you out celebrating?"

She lifted her drink, tipped it to his, and took a sip. "I am," she said.

The look he gave her now wasn't exactly *sad* but it wasn't particularly cheerful either. "Sometimes," he finally spoke. "Sometimes you have to bump around in the dark before you find where you're really going."

Her brow furrowed, trying to decipher this runic statement. His accent was intriguing. She took another sip. "*Da dove Lei viene in Italia?*" ("Where do you come from in Italy?"). The words sprang out before she could stop them. This time her pink tinge was earned embarrassment.

"*Parl' l'Italian' abbastanz' be.'*" ("You speak Italian well.") the man said, and then went on with a very long and flowery sentence she lost track of after the first few words. He cocked his head to appraise her. "*Abbesuogno mmece parl' Nupelitan'.*" The words were harsh and soft at the same time.

"What?" she asked.

"You should be speaking Neapolitan instead," he translated. "You are Greco-Italiano."

"Did Sammie tell you my name is Greco?" she demanded.

"He didn't," he shrugged. "But it only makes sense." Meeting her eyes, he answered. "Your nose and your hair—and," he added, "the fire in your eyes."

Lisa's nose was straight and embarrassingly longer than she'd have liked it, with a slight curl-up at the end that made her the target of many a grade school joke. Her jet-black hair rippled with natural waves as though it had been permanently permed at the fanciest salon in Manhattan. The older she got the less she liked the way she looked. One rainy day she removed all the mirrors from her Brooklyn apartment. That made her feel better.

She glanced at the bar mirror to confirm that her blush had deepened. She'd gone and done the unthinkable, blurting out a few coherent words of a language she loved but had not nearly mastered—leaving her in a pickle that left no alternative but confession. "I'd love to speak Italian well, and Neapolitan even more," she said, "but I kind of developed a block. I learned a few words from my grandfather just before he died. But I got so much grief from my parents I found it harder and harder to speak their native language. It's one of my biggest regrets. Babbino was going to teach me properly when I came home from college. Instead my first trip home was for his funeral." That's what you get when you love somebody too much, she reflected. At the same moment she felt her shoulders relax, she brushed her eyes with the back of her hand.

"You've never been in Italy?" the tall man not so much asked as intoned with the tenor of a Requiem Mass. He shook his head as her eyes responded.

"That is to my shame," she said, her face darkening again. Her skin was so pale she'd been called porcelain more than once. Which only aggravated the blushes.

"What part of Italy was your grandfather from?" he prodded gently.

"Somewhere north of Naples," she said. "An ancient town in Campania, Pozz—" She hesitated.

"Pozzuoli," he finished for her.

"Yes, exactly. Near there."

The old man's eyes shone with a light she'd never witnessed before, but one she recognized deep in her bones. "*Anch'io*," he said simply. "I am too. A long time ago."

"Do you go back to visit?"

He shook his head. "I can never go back. Not as long as my brother is alive. I did something he cannot forgive me for." He paused, steeling his gaze. "You will go there," he said. "You will feel the magic. You will say your rosary. Then you will decide."

"How do you know what I need to decide?"

The man's eyes twinkled with nostalgia. "How can you accept any future without learning your past?"

Two

LISA TOOK HER TIME GETTING into work the next day, stopping on her way to the train to have her nails done. She had them painted clear instead of her usual brown. When the manicurist offered her a ten-minute neck massage, she pampered herself and assented. Funny how two operations so simple could make her feel so civilized, so in control.

When Lisa got to Manhattan, noticing that it was already eight-thirty, a half hour later than her usual arrival, she still didn't resist her favorite delicatessen on Broadway and stopped for "the usual two to go." After all, in the daring mood she was in, what difference did it make if she was "late" for work—although she well knew her contract clearly stated that she had full discretion over the length of her office day. Normally, this kind of self-indulgence was unheard of. Normally, what made her feel whole and in charge was to be in the office before her self-proclaimed rivals. Not today. Her meeting with Kevin's boss was at ten o'clock. Sitting in her office fidgeting at her desk for two hours wasn't Lisa's idea of a sane prelude to a meeting that could determine her fate. So she even sat at the deli window bar to sip an espresso before continuing.

The frothy zigzag on its surface beckoned her attention, like a crystal ball capable of showing her past, present, and future. She hesitated before taking the first sip that would disrupt the design the barista had drawn with foam. She loved zigzag. To take that sip she must disturb its simple perfection, and whatever omen she might read in it. That was one of life's many ironies: moving into any future leaves the present behind.

How can I accept any future without understanding my past? After his oddly resonant pronouncement last night, the stranger had disappeared. She'd just excused herself to visit the ladies' room, was there fewer than five minutes. But the dapper man who'd done "something unforgivable" long ago was nowhere to be seen when she returned. She gave Sammie a perplexed look, nodding her head to the stool he'd used, which was now occupied by a woman in a very sexy cocktail dress and perfume as heavy as her makeup. Sammie's frown was equally perplexed, a wrinkled look that said, "I don't know what you're talking about." That annoyed her, so she made the universal air-scrawl that meant, "Bring me my check." His frown this time was accompanied with a hand signal that said, "No check required. It's been taken care of," then: "Sorry we couldn't talk tonight. Next time!"

She left hurriedly, after leaving a twenty dollar bill. She was grateful for the more than brisk air that encountered her outside and the frigid tail wind that pursued her two-block walk home. She remembered feeling unusually giddy and not being able to figure out how much was due to the alcohol, how much to the conversation, how much to the events of the day, and how much to the exhilaration of being warm against the harsh elements inside the black pea coat she'd treated herself to after her last raise.

Taking that first sip shattered the foamy zigzag. Affording her a sudden unruly glimpse into the emotional flatness of her straight-line course through Yale to the publishing seminar to her present treadmill life at Standard House. A publisher that had, last year, merged with another equally distinguished company. That seemed to be the pattern these days of insatiable corporate cannibalism. Where there was once some forty "majors," there were eventually only six, depending on how you counted. With last year's merger, the six became five and houses that used to be independently revered and literarily powerful—Bantam, Doubleday, Ballantine, Crown, Berkeley, Touchstone, Dutton, Farrar Strauss, Free Press, Pocket, Pocket Books, Random House, Scribner's—were now mere "imprints," ghosts of their own history, jammed together under conglomerate umbrellas named Hachette Livre, Holtzbrinck, CBS, Penguin Random House. With each implosion of one star system into another, the resulting black holes characteristically displayed themselves in more power for the marketing folk, and less for the editorial. Accountability shifted even further from literary accolades toward bottom-line profits. The idealism with which Lisa's "career in letters" began had, year by year, been forced to gasp for breath in a secret cave in the back of her mind, while she ploughed daily through manuscripts, mostly ghostwritten, by celebrity names from Hollywood, the music world, D.C. politics, haute couture, or the Fortune 100 list.

The handful of heartwarming or thought-provoking novels or inspiring books of nonfiction that she used to be allowed to acquire, like the ones she'd once dreamed of writing, were allowed today only a minuscule fragment of her attention. North American rights to Elsa Ferrante's novels like Marsha Sinetar's *Ordinary People as Monks and Mystics,* much as she loved them, were just collateral damage to changing times. When she pitched one of her "darlings," she was tap-dancing her soul away before automatons. Acquiring a new voice, while still technically possible, had become a twice-a-year event at best—and one that always came with a sharp reminder that she was risking her career by going to the mat for a book she believed in. "Grow up," she told herself. "Things change. The world changes. You can't argue with progress." She laughed, remembering a line from Kurt Vonnegut, Jr.'s *Sirens of Titan:* "Every passing hour brings the Solar System forty-three thousand miles closer to Globular Cluster M13 in Hercules — and still there are some misfits who insist that there is no such thing as progress." She wondered if Vonnegut-before-he-was-Vonnegut could get accepted by a major publisher today. She shook her head—causing the people around her to throw surreptitious glances her way. Kurt would probably direct-publish and throw his fate with Amazon, trusting he'd discover his readers directly, gatekeepers be damned.

She wondered how soon functionaries like herself would become extinct.

Lisa's mind moved back to the present moment, which, tingling with the excitement of uncertainty, was as mysterious as it could be. She was savoring every last minute, as though she were facing execution.

Finally, she stood up, rebuttoned her coat, and headed like the good soldier she was across the wind-whipped street to confront her fate.

Three

HER INCOMING PILE WAS EXACTLY high enough that the sorting and opening would easily fill up the time remaining before the dread encounter. She laughed at her hyperbole. "You're so dramatic," her mother had scolded her regularly. "You'd think it was the end of the world. It's not."

She also needed to catch up with emails from Larry Thompson, whose social thrillers were becoming successful enough for her to flag for Standard and whose new book, his first from Standard, was about to appear; and from Joan Angsten, her first New York Times bestseller who was demanding more and more of her attention lately. What would Joan do without me? she asked herself. Her latest email was an outpouring of frustration at Standard's insistence that she cut down her new manuscript to 100,000. "Where in the annals of literature did anyone set that number as sacred?" she wanted to know. "Good question," Lisa responded. "Welcome to the brave new world where every page costs money to produce and directly affects the R.O.I." But it was also true that books today were trending shorter because readers' attention span was continuing to fall into synch with the advent of texting and tweeting. Lisa observed herself making that argument as though from on high, and wondered exactly when that part of her brain had joined the nouveau establishment. But she also knew Joan adored her.

When she looked up at the wall clock, the appointed hour had come.

Phyllis Graham, pushing sixty-five, had a face as smooth as an android straight off the assembly line. She opened without preliminaries: "We'd like you to move into Kevin's position, beginning immediately."

Lisa's eyebrows went up, not being sure what kind of response was appropriate.

Obviously that didn't matter to Ms. Graham. "Your salary would start at $160, subject to annual review, and your bonuses, of course, will be tied to the number of bestsellers you generate each year, plus those achieved by your editorial staff."

Lisa was confounded by such an instant change of fortune. *Your* staff! And surely she couldn't mean $160,000? That was an unimaginable jump from her present pay-grade, which had put the once upon a time dream of owning her own condo into deep hold. Although the iron fist was still in her belly, something deep inside was beginning to feel real good, as though life had justified her career choice—against all those jeering Eli classmates heading for law, business, medicine, dentistry, and pharmacology. They called her a wild-eyed dreamer.

Graham curtly brought her back to reality. "Well," the publisher demanded, looking at her wrist as though she were wearing a watch. "What do you have to say?"

"I need some time," Lisa heard herself saying, self-consciously turning her own watch on its fraying black leather band.

"Some time? Okay, sure. Shall we say same time tomorrow, unless you can make it earlier?"

"I'm sorry," Lisa answered. "There's something I need to do for myself first," she added by way of lame explanation.

Graham's stare showed she was edging toward annoyance. She was a busy woman, with lots of fish to fry, fires to put out—who'd just offered a promising rookie a chance to skip five or more years of further plodding advancement to experience immediate management development and untold opportunity. "What do you have in mind?" she finally asked.

"I need to go to Italy first." The words fumbled their way out of her brain and into the air.

Graham's look was sheer disbelief. "Excuse me," she said. "I couldn't have heard you correctly."

"I've never been," she stammered. "I mean, it's something I need to do for myself."

Graham cut her short. "Fine," she said. "Go for two weeks, and we'll hold the position open. When you're back I'll need a decision before we can move forward." She looked at the wall calendar. "It's October 13. I'll expect you back in this office November 1. Take the rest of the day off. Meanwhile, I'm assuming a positive decision.'" Her sentence trailed off into dismissiveness.

Lisa stood up. "Okay," she said. "And, Ms. Graham, thank you for the honor of considering me. Thank you for everything. I am really grateful."

Was that a snort she heard as she walked out the door?

Four

BORN INTO A SOUTHERN ITALIAN immigrant family in Buffalo, the moment she reached "the age of reason," as the Catholics quaintly called it, Lisa Greco started counting the days before she could permanently escape the deep-frozen little city. She'd never earned the right to be called "a good Catholic girl," the highest accolade achievable in the ethnic enclave.

But being a "good girl" was hers by default—facilitated by the fact that boys found her too skinny, her nose too long, and her chest too flat.

She'd been a bad Catholic, allergic to incense and guitars. Her rebellion against the Roman Catholic Church reached a crux the day of her Confirmation, when she realized she couldn't reconcile the deeply moving beliefs expressed in the liturgy with the way so many Catholics—not to mention priests and bishops—actually behaved.

She vowed from that sacramental day that hypocrisy would be her enemy, and when she got nowhere pointing it out out loud, she started writing about it. Writing would be her true identity, by which she separated herself from the world.

In high school at Sacred Heart Academy, Lisa rebelled against subjects she didn't excel at. But she exceled at Latin, Greek, and English—and, half way through her sophomore year, started taking college classes in the classics and Italian at nearby Villa Maria. There she studied Homer, Virgil, Herodotus, and Early Renaissance Italian—falling in love with Dante, then with the ribald stories of Boccaccio. She determined to learn Italian more fully one day, especially because her memory of her family's Neapolitan was fading, confusing, and troubled.

One cold winter morning she returned home from school to discover that she'd won the Danforth Fellowship.

A phone call from an admissions officer told her that her place on Yale University's waiting list had, overnight, solidified.

She was the only one in her small class to be "going to Yale on a Danforth."

Her Yale literature professors were world-renowned. But Lisa found herself spending more time in the Sterling Library than in their classrooms or in her claustrophobic room in Calhoun College. In addition to churning out one "Honors" term paper after another, including a diatribe on the subject of John C. Calhoun's lifelong apologia for slavery that got the attention of the whole university and was published online without her knowledge or permission and gleaned over 20,000 reads, she went on to write for both the *Yale Daily News* and the *Yale Literary Magazine*. She was torn between being a crusading journalist, a novelist, or an editor. But her father, when she'd announced she was majoring in literature, had responded: "What will you do for a living?" So much for novelist. Then, as the presidential election churned on for nearly her entire junior and senior years, she became progressively sickened by the cynically corporate face that journalism was offering to the world.

So when she spotted, in the hallways of Hopper—the new name for Calhoun College, honoring computer pioneer Grace Murray Hopper—a notice for the Yale Publishing Course being offered in the summer following her graduation, she decided to throw her fate into the hands of serendipity—and signed up.

From there, Lisa entered the maelstrom. Her life was no longer her own. After the intense week of the publishing course, she had her very first Metropolitan at a cocktail party filled with senior editors who had trekked up by Metro-North from Manhattan to fall upon the course's innocent graduates like a pride of lions attacking a herd of baby gazelle.

Because of her straight Honors in all courses literary, and despite her mediocre grades in science and math—she'd gotten through math by talking her prof into letting her write a paper on "the history of numbers" instead of taking the final exam she knew she'd fail—Lisa was offered jobs by four of the five biggest publishing houses.

Since the offers were all about the same financially, it was easy to choose Standard. For one thing, Kevin Boyle was charming. He impressed her not because he'd taken the trouble to research her thoroughly, but by his intuition. "I know you're a bit young to make a decision like this," he said. "But look at it this way. It's an opportunity to live and work in the most powerful city in the world, among highly intelligent and dedicated people, doing what you love best, reading—and writing." He didn't mention that the writing would be endless reports, book analyses, and Profit-Loss statements. She had to admit it all sounded exotic—and exciting—to an ambitious gal from provincial Buffalo. And they will pay me to do this? Her father would have been proud of her.

Learn the business of writing first-hand. And not starve in a garret. Worst case, she concluded, it will buy time for me to figure myself out, figure out what I was really meant to do in life.

It didn't quite turn out that way. Does it ever? Lisa wasn't left with much time to figure out anything big-picture. She quickly became the consummate micromanager, reading or at least skimming three or four manuscripts—ranging from 30,000 word short stories to 600,000 word prose epics—every day. On her commute, on her "lunch break" while nibbling a randomly-chosen Prêt-A-Manger sandwich. Sometimes her eyes were so intently focused on the iPad screen she didn't have time to even look at her food—and when she'd finished sometimes couldn't even remember which sandwich she'd gobbled down. With any luck, the subway knocked out two of the manuscripts. She wouldn't read past fifty pages if she wasn't fully on board with the story or the writing by that point. She'd deal with finishing the third manuscript in bed, forcing her eyes to remain open until she reached a determination on it.

Work days were a solid blur of activity: sorting endless mail, pitch lunches with agents, editorial meetings, marketing meetings, acquisition meetings that were a hapless mix of editorial and marketing with marketing playing the key role.

Her stress increased, her social life became a joke, and her few moments of decompression came only at Sammie's Bar or Starbucks.

When Sammie asked her casually one night how "her love life was," she almost coughed down her drink. What did that even mean? Other than serving as platonic escort to one of her married male bosses forced to attend a banquet or fête-the-author command performance, or dancing a few perfunctory rounds at a classmate's Upstate, Connecticut, or Long Island wedding, her contact with men would have made her target fodder for *New York Magazine's* personals—if she'd had the time to work them. Which she assuredly did not. Her mother, had she had the opportunity, would have warned her shrilly of impending spinsterhood.

It just wasn't fair for her to be offered her boss's position now. So soon. While her recruitment from Yale had seemed to her kind of random, this promotion seemed definitively life-changing. It came without warning. Kevin had once told her, when she asked him how many years he intended to stay at it, "Until they cart me away," and quoted Benjamin Franklin: 'There's nothing wrong with retirement as long as it does not interfere with a man's work." Larry Thompson consoled her that life was a journey, not a destination. Well, she wasn't sure Standard was her life's destination.

Five

CLIMBING THE STAIRS FROM THE station in Park Slope, Lisa heard the tell-tale chirp that proclaimed voicemail. She was a puppet, whose controlling strings were voicemails, emails, and texts.

Actually it was two voicemails, both of them unexpected. The first was from Phyllis Graham's executive assistant: "Ms. Graham wants you to call 212-256-0850, Voyages Unlimited, and make your travel arrangements through them. The full expense will be on the company," she ended, hanging up without further explanation. Wow, Lisa thought. She'd never been treated like royalty by anyone in her life, least of all by Standard.

The second voicemail was from Sammie at the bar. "Drop by tonight," he said. "I owe you a drink, and a chat. Sorry about the other night. It was too crazy. Besides," he added. "I have something for you." *That* was certainly intriguing. What was going on? She felt like her life was spinning out of control and she wasn't sure she liked it.

Rooting through her dresser, she saw that her passport had more than a year left on it and it didn't take long to book her reservations with Unlimited. She'd last used the passport to go to a sales conference in Cancun—the only young editor not to have brought a bikini. She was just too far behind on her reading, and was determined to stay on her balcony and get it done. She booked New York to Rome, startled that the agency insisted on a seat in business class. They also took care of the train from Rome's Leonardo da Vinci Airport straight to Napoli. In a moment of resurgent responsibility, she told them to book the return trip for October 31 so she could be back to work November 1. They crisply informed her that they'd already done that.

Then she headed for Sammie's. She glanced at her phone as she entered and noticed it was already eight-thirty. She hoped she hadn't waited so long that the bar would be jammed again.

Instead, the place was nearly empty—three people at the counter that seated twenty, and only one couple at the tables. Sammie, wearing his usual t-shirt and vest, greeted her with a smile. "Hey, how's my favorite patron?" He nodded for her to take the nearest stool. He walked over. "The usual four Metropolitans?"

She laughed ruefully. What had possessed her the other night? Two was her limit, and she rarely made it through the second. "Tonight I'll start with one, thank you," she said.

Sammie concocted her libation with dispatch, and returned to set the drink in front of her on a napkin. "On the house," he said. "I understand congratulations are in order," he added.

Her look showed her surprise. "How do you know that?"

"It's a bartender's job to know things," he winked. "Besides, I have a grapevine that winds all the way to Manhattan."

She took a sip of her drink before giving him a demanding look. "I'm leaving for Italy tomorrow. Can you believe it?"

His thumbs up showed his approval. "Atta girl," he said. "Which reminds me." He reached into his vest pocket and placed a small, flat gold key-like object in her hand. "Your friend from the other night came back after you'd left and insisted I give this to you.

He said, 'Tell her it will help focus the miracle. But don't forget to say that rosary.'"

She rolled her eyes. Then, staring at the object, her heart nearly stopped. It was a gold pendant with a zigzag-like design stamped into it. Only it wasn't exactly a zigzag; it was exactly the design of her grandfather's cufflinks that she'd lost in New Haven—or that a roommate had stolen from her there. They were the only sentimental  things she'd brought with her to college, a gift from her Babbino to "remember" him. He called the design "the Greek key," what looked like miniature labyrinths. She was familiar with the labyrinth from her classical studies—a shape that most resembled her mind. And its weathered look told her it was quite old. "I don't get it," she said. "What's it for? And what miracle?"

Sammie looked as perplexed as she was. "I thought *you* would tell *me*," he said. "I wasn't part of that conversation, remember? When I asked him that, he just smiled at me. 'She needs to find out for herself.' He handed me this beat-up card. Those were his parting words, and he was out the door." Sammie handed the card to her. It looked like it had been carried in the same wallet for a century, but the words were still clear:

Hotel la Tripergola

Via Miliscola, 165, 80078 Pozzuoli NA, Italy

Phone: +39 081 421 0256

"Who was that guy anyway?" she asked. "You're not trying to hook me up, are you? It looks like real gold. I can't accept this."

Sammie shrugged. "Shall I toss it for you?" He reached for it.

But Lisa wasn't letting go yet.

"Seriously, I have no idea who he was," was Sammie's sincere answer. "I never saw him before that night."

His answer baffled her. "He was sure nostalgic for Italy. If you didn't know him why did you send him over to talk to me?"

"I sent him over to the empty stool next to you—the only one left at the bar that night. I handed him your drink. 'Take this to the lady with the serious look,' I said."

Lisa had no idea what to think. It didn't quite synch with how she remembered the evening—but little of her recent life was feeling as orderly and humdrum as it had before the last few days. She took another sip of the Metropolitan and was already contemplating having another. She realized she was clutching the stranger's gift in her hand, and let herself relax enough to tuck it safely into her purse. She loved mysteries. Now she had a mission: to find out what the pendant meant. In a land she'd never before visited.

Six

THE NEXT MORNING PASSED LIKE lightning. Before she knew it she'd breezed through check-in at JFK, negotiated TSA precheck, and was boarding United Flight 40 to Rome. She dressed for comfort and, as always, not to draw attention to herself. Faded jeans with no holes, her usual black-framed "librarian" glasses as bartender Sammie called them, and a gray Yale sweatshirt.

She'd selected the only available window seat in business, since all the aisle seats were already spoken for. She got settled and firmly pulled the shade down. There was nothing she wanted to see during takeoff. Flying made her nervous, not to mention her latent claustrophobia. With her lame performance in high school physics and Cs in algebra and geometry, she never really mastered the basic principles of aerodynamics. That a five hundred thousand pound Airbus could stay in the air she found a preposterous and slightly untrustworthy exception to Newton's laws. The less she witnessed of the whole experiment, the better.

Fortunately the passengers within eye-reach were mostly visiting Chinese mainlanders who'd done a two-day shopping layover in New York en route to invading Rome. They would provide no threat to her mental space. Lisa pulled out her iPad reader and switched it on. But after a half page of the next submission in her endless queue, she recalled her promise to minimize Standard work.

She switched to the Neapolitan guidebook she'd downloaded this morning. She was fascinated to learn that Naples was one of the main incubators of Italian literature. The history of the Neapolitan language was deeply affected by the rising importance of Dante Alighieri's Tuscan dialect; her other favorite Tuscan poet and novelist, Giovanni Boccaccio, lived for years at the court of Naples' King Robert of Anjou, known as Robert the Wise. Boccaccio used Naples as one of the settings for his *Decameron;* his works were also notable for containing a sprinkling of Neapolitan words. When the Spanish invaded Naples in 1734, Alfonso of Aragon ruled that official documents be written in Neapolitan instead of Latin. Later Spanish was to replace Neapolitan.

Despite her good night's sleep, Lisa's eyes were getting heavy. After a glance at her wristwatch to see if they were late departing, she was asleep before the plane took off.

Her dark eyes flashed open to the flight attendant offering her a warm towel. "Business class could be addictive," she said to herself. She stretched, tried to read the guidebook again, but gave it up when her tomato juice was delivered. She wasn't here to read; she was here to write. She pulled out her tablet instead. Happily enough, she did feel the urge and began, tentatively, to sketch out a novel, one that *she* would want to read.

Seven

LEONARDO DA VINCI AIRPORT, LIKE so many U.S. airports, was "under construction," a haphazardly-draped-with-murky-plastic super-modern steel-ribbed structure being erected on the back of the old Fiumicino. She threw herself into the mad rush of too many diverse humans swarming toward too many different destinations, as though an ant hill had just lost its queen and the workers were scrambling around without direction.

By the time she arrived at the carousel her bag was already down. She grabbed it with the help of a handsome teenager who sprang to her aid. Getting through customs was a breeze. Clearly the European Union was still determined to make visitors and their cash welcome. She just had time to text Kevin: "I'm in Rome. Hard to believe!"

Then she followed the instructions she'd copied from the Internet to weave her way to the train platform. She had an hour and a half transit, so she stopped at the first elegant coffee bar she ran across, and ordered a cappuccino from the uniformed barista who sprang into action and served her with cool professionalism and an appraising glance. The coffee was exquisite, and revived her from the long trip.

A text arrived back from Kevin: "Take your time. Savor. Hurry back. Keep your eye on Sunday's Book Review."

So like Kevin. So like New Yorkers. "Relax," someone tells them. "How long?" they respond, eyeing their watches.

And she'd be damned if she was going to check the *New York Times* this Sunday. *This* Sunday she'd be in another world.

"*La signorina vuole altro?*" ("Would the signorina like something else?") the barista was asking.

"*No, grazie,*" she managed to get the words out without stammering. "*Sono bona.*"

He nodded and moved away.

She felt a surge of triumph. Step by step, word by word, she'd figure it out. And she'd figure out her life too.

She marched resolutely for the train to Naples. Eminem's "Lose Yourself" was blaring from the station loudspeakers, no doubt to motivate the crisscrossing travelers. The song always made her edgy. She *was* losing herself, just not in the way he meant. A vendor offering colorful scarves caught her eye. Of the grand total of three scarves to her name, all of them were black or gray. Without hesitating, she pointed to a bright purple one and confronted the vendor. "*Quanto costa quella?*"

She was impressed to discover that her designated conveyance was an ultra-modern maroon and gray-striped bullet train imprinted with a green and red logo made from the letters "F.S.," for "*Ferrovie dello Stato Italiane*" ("Italian National Railroad").

The train departed exactly at the 2:05 dictated by the timetable.

Her seat was perfectly comfortable, but it faced backward. She didn't like traveling backwards. She spotted seats facing forward at the other end of the car, found an empty one, and settled in. *This* was much better. Now she could look forward to where she was going.

Lisa folded the scarf and tucked it into her satchel, then settled back and watched the distant domes and spires of Rome give way to sprawling modern suburbs every bit as unsightly as New York's. As the train glided smoothly along, urban sprawl quickly gave way to elegant cypresses, ancient orchards, and yellowing vineyards surrounded with stone walls and tended by stone cottages that looked like they'd been tending for thousands of years.

A porter pushed a tray of beverages down the aisle toward her. He offered her a choice of coffee, mineral water, or an orange-colored cocktail in a San Pellegrino bottle. Feeling celebratory for having navigated this far, she asked for the orange bottle and watched him flip the cap off expertly and pour it into a plastic cup for her. "*Salute,*" he said.

The sunny drink was surprisingly light and delicious. She loved its bitter-sweet flavor. "*Come si chiamano quelli arbori con foglie di argento?*" ("What are those trees with silver leaves called?") she asked the porter.

He cocked his head to see where she was pointing, and gave her a skeptical look. "*Olive,*" he answered.

She pulled out her iPad. It seemed imperative that she should record every new sensation, and the words for it, in this land that had given birth to her grandfather.

Eight

TIME FLEW BY AS LISA sipped the Pellegrino and jotted her observations: the contrast of greens and yellows in the fields, highlands on the horizon, the sense of lazy ease as the train moved south from Rome, her growing sense of peace the farther she got from New York—and from Standard.

She fingered the gold pendant and reflected on her habit of zigzagging through the streets of Manhattan. If she had to go from 54th and Broadway to 33rd and Lexington, she'd walk a block down Broadway to 53rd, then turn left and walk to 7th Avenue, down 7th to a left on 52nd, then right on Avenue of the Americas to Radio City Music Hall, left on 50th, right on 5th Avenue, until she reached her destination—hating it when she ran out of turns and had to walk the last few blocks straight down the same street. Why the indirection? She loved the serendipity of seeing things she'd never have seen if she'd moved in long right angles. She felt like she was exploring her options, commanding the map as her own, allowing a little adventure in an otherwise straight-ahead life. But could it really be, as a therapist she visited one time suggested, that she really saw her life as a labyrinth and was bent on finding the right path through it while also keeping alternatives open? Sheesh. She knew what had started as a habit had now become imprinted. She was incapable, even when with someone else, of walking two blocks in a row at the outset. She'd shaped her brain around the habit as surely as flossing or washing her face.

The recorded P.A. system announced "Napoli Centrale" before she knew it, and Lisa was quick to stand up and head for the end of the car to release her suitcase from the clever cable-lock that secured it. A crush of passengers were already cluttering the exit, but Lisa reminded herself she was in no hurry. As the ultra-modern doors slid open, she waited for the crush to dissolve before pulling her luggage down the steps onto the concrete platform.

She'd traveled light—only the one gray suitcase and her black leather shoulder purse, which, mindful of warnings issued by her Manhattan associates, she strapped around her neck so she could carry it in front of her. On the platform a tall gray-haired porter approached her and gestured to take her bag. She thanked him, but shook her head firmly. "*Non ho bisogno di aiuto, grazie,*" she said, "I don't need help, thank you."

The station was nestled between banks of rose-colored apartment buildings, its platforms covered by ultra-modern umbrella-like steel struts that were delightfully practical and stylish at the same time. She could see the passengers slowing as they walked toward the terminal, as though shedding the frantic pace of Rome. Rush was no longer necessary here. Walking in time with them it still took Lisa only a few minutes to join the arrivals buzzing around the taxi stand. Things moved efficiently, and before she knew it she was climbing into a sparkling-clean multi-colored taxi. She glanced over her shoulder at the mountains looming in the distance—two peaks, one slighter lower than the other. They glistened in the sun their welcome.

The driver smiled at her in his rearview mirror. "*Salve,*" he acknowledged. "*Lei dove va?*" ("Where are you going?") The ancient word *Salve* gave her a thrill. The last time she'd seen it was in high school Latin class, where she encountered it in a lyric by Catullus: *"Salve atque vale,"* "Hello and goodbye." So the Roman imperial greeting was still in use here.

Lisa gave him a businesslike but friendly glance, and returned his smile. She waved the scrap of paper she was clutching in her first. "Via Toledo *due cento cinque*," she said crisply. "Via Toledo 205." She'd learned enough to know that the key to Italian was articulating every syllable.

The driver nodded. *"Jamma jà—duj' ciento cinch'"* ("Let's go—205"), he said in the harsh-soft language of Naples, not bothering to glance at the paper. With a decisive lurch from the taxi line, they were off to the races, the car slicing through traffic as though it were coated with Teflon.

She settled back to take in a swirl of colors—multi-hued pastels of buildings, bright yellows and reds of cars and pedestrians. The driver pointed out *Castel Nuovo,* its massive stones perfectly intact despite the six hundred years they'd weathered. He pointed out so many monuments displayed for her admiration on the city's surrounding hilltops as they passed them that Lisa couldn't possibly keep track of them all. She sank back comfortably and let impressions slide over her.

Nine

HER GOOGLE MAP SHOWED THE Airbnb she'd booked was very close to the station, but the ride took twenty minutes. At first it occurred to her to question the driver, who'd asked her, *"Lei è americana?"* the moment she'd spoken. But she checked herself, realizing that the duration of the ride was dictated by the endless one-way streets.

Finally they were turning uphill from the harbor, where humongous modern ocean liners seemed out of place at the stately ancient wharfs, and onto cobblestoned Santa Brigida. Her host, Fabio, had informed her when she'd called from the train that Via Toledo, where his flat would be found, was a *zona pedonale* so that she'd have to be deposited at the corner and walk "a few meters" to the door of his palazzo. It sounded like a ways, but she didn't mind. She was a New Yorker, quite used to walking miles if not quite used to meters.

She no doubt cut a funny figure, an obviously newly-arrived American tourist, dragging her big suitcase, clutching her purse in front of her, and juggling her cell phone at the same time because it was chirping that she had a text. But the strollers that filled Via Toledo, lost in their conversations, barely gave her a glance. The text was from Ms. Graham: "Thompson made the list." Lisa grunted and turned off the damned phone. So she'd earned another notch on her belt. Yippee.

The walk was less than a minute—past perfume and pastry, clothing and shoe shops named "Swarovski," "Pepino," "Passions de Soft L.U.I.S.E," "Zara," "Carpisa"—before she found herself in front of an immensely wide and weather-beaten green door to a faded-pink stucco building. The plaque announced in white letters on a dusk-rose background: *"Palazzo Domenico Barbaja, residenza di Giuseppe Rossini, 1815-22."*

How cool is that? she thought.

The street scene was so happy, colorful, and musical that she regretted the walk was so quick. Maybe she could sit at the little piazza across the street and watch the world go by for a while. The pedestrians seemed content walking and chatting. Very few wore earbuds.

But her luggage made her mindful of warnings from her street-savvy friends. She closed the distance to the door quickly.

As she moved to ring the bell, the green door swung open on its own. Two young women exited, both wearing holey jeans and brightly-colored pullovers, so deep in conversation they were oblivious to the travel-weary Amerigana facing them. Lisa lifted her bag over the metal lintel, then stepped over it, and found herself in the dark cool shadows of an ample courtyard. In contrast to the busy merriment of the avenue, the courtyard embodied the serenity of a convent cloister. Now she understood why the huge shabby door was forbidding and unattractive—that was its protective guise.

She surveyed the lofty interior. The courtyard was built in the center of stacked balconies looking out from the individual staircases that led to them, so that the residents of each floor could peer out at arriving guests unseen. When her eyes had adjusted to the gloom, Lisa spotted the diminutive elevator shaft was nestled in front of a small office that featured a bustling fish tank and a sleeping guard.

The arthritic lift took its time arriving from on high. Lisa wrangled open the heavy steel door and clambered in—just enough room for her and the suitcase. What looked like a collection box on the car's wall puzzled her. She tried pushing "5," the top button. The Airbnb photos had boasted views that could only have been from the roof. When the elevator creaked its way up to the top floor, she nudged it open with her hip, dragged the suitcase out, and faced a winding flight of stone steps—not many, but steep.

Halfway through her climb, Fabio appeared out of thin air. He grabbed her suitcase as though it were filled with feathers and escorted her to the flat's entrance doorway at the top of the stairs. "Sorry," he said in more than passable English. "You're a little earlier than I expected. I was still at the pool."

His smile was dazzling, muscles rippling from his cut-off shirt, and he was indeed well-tanned as though pools were his natural habitat.

He led Lisa across an ample wood-planked courtyard with a table and chairs on both sides—one facing the commanding steel cupola of the "Galleria Umberto," the others facing two-mounded Mount Vesuvius.

"Wow," she said, "what great views."

Fabio was all business as he led her down a hallway with several other doors, to her rental at the end. It was guarded by a coat rack that looked like it might have served the Roman Empire. He opened the door for her and handed her a set of keys. One, he recited, for the street door, one for the courtyard, and the last for the apartment itself. He also pointed to the bowl at the courtyard entrance filled with ten-Euro-cents pieces. "For the elevator," he said, "before and after work hours." That explained the coin box. He handed her his card, gave her another head to toe appraisal, saluted with a wave of his hand and a rascally wink, and urged her to contact him if she needed "anything at all." Then, as suddenly as he'd appeared, he vanished—and she was alone.

She surveyed her new domain and saw that it was good: three quite spacious rooms—kitchen, bedroom, and bathroom—plus the "private balcony off the bedroom." Each room was painted its own bright cheerful color: red bathroom, blue bedroom, and yellow kitchen. She opened the French doors—their voile curtains just opaque enough for privacy—to discover her balcony was equipped with a slatted wood table and two sturdy wooden chairs.

She sat down to take in the view and sounds from the street below. The snatch of music she'd heard on the walk from the taxi lifted her heart immediately with its bell-like clarity: "*Funiculi! Funiculà!*" The melody would be running through her brain incessantly now. Peering over the wrought-iron rail she finally located the source of the roughhewn tenor sound: a tall older man with gray-white hair standing in the middle of the bustling street waving his arms as though he were Pavarotti. His voice was pretty damned good. He was accompanied by a hard-working violinist. The two musicians had transformed pedestrians into onlookers, onlookers into happily clapping audience. Three teenagers linked arms and were skipping to the familiar tune:

Jammo, jammo 'ncoppa jammo jà
Jammo, jammo 'ncoppa jammo jà

Lisa couldn't take her eyes off the scene. She had no idea what the words meant, but they made her smile and want to dance. It had to be Neapolitan. She would Google the words later. She hummed the music. A memory from childhood flashed through her mind:

Dream boy, dream boy, where's the boy for me?

What was that all about? An image from a pre-teen "mixer" at her childhood parish house. Yikes, she was losing it. She turned her attention away from the street and gazed at the impressive fortress on the large hill in front of her. The view calmed her. Its majestic serenity made her feel lucky to be alive. Then she noticed the blue ladder.

It was encircled by a steel cage that would make the thin rungs safer to climb. She couldn't resist, and soon found herself staring onto the terrace she'd seen in the Airbnb photos. She scrambled the last few steps and climbed over the stucco parapet and onto the terracotta pavement.

The terrace was perfect for taking in the view—the hillside fortress of Sant'Elmo on one side, Vesuvius on the other—and on a third side she could make out the Bay of Naples surprisingly close by. She took in a deep breath of appreciation. A private paradise all her own. She could envision herself meditating here, with no worries of interruption and the sheer bliss of the warm and friendly air. She could envision herself lying on the wood-slat chaise longue basking in the bright Neapolitan sun. She did a little dance around the table, wondering how she'd manage to bring food up here to picnic beneath the bright blue sky and puffy white clouds. She felt a clash of desires—wanting to remain in this beautiful place in solitude forever, and wanting to run out into the streets and explore every inch of this city that was welcoming her with love songs.

She climbed down the blue ladder carefully, then went inside to check out the bathroom—complete with a bidet and glass shower cage. In the kitchen-dining room a bright red espresso pot stood at attention on the stove. A blue ceramic container marked *Caffè* was filled with dark brown powder that smelled heavenly. She checked the cabinets, and the sparkling clean refrigerator. Clearly a shopping expedition was called for. Despite her travel-weariness, she grabbed the keys and her bag, and headed out through the courtyard, remembering to grab two ten-Euro-cent coins from the accommodating bowl before heading down the stone steps.

The elevator door didn't slide shut when she pushed "1," so she dropped a coin in the offering box. That did the job. The coin clicked to join the pile of others and the mechanical counter clanged once to announce "245,338" like a miserly odometer.

The courtyard remained cool and inviting. But she was on a beeline for the big world beyond the green door.

Ten

LISA NORMALLY GAVE WIDE BERTH to Fifth Avenue or Times Square, or anywhere packed with crowds. Outside the green door she didn't notice any tourists on crowded Via Toledo, but her eyes were immediately drawn across the wide boulevard to an ancient stone staircase leading upward from the far side of the small square. She headed instinctively for the staircase, just because it disappeared into shadows and beckoned mysterious.

As she climbed, she noticed that even graffiti here looked laid-back and cheerful—not the angry and drug-hyped scrawling of the rampaging gangs of New York.

Via Speranzella at the top of the stairs was a traffic-worn contrast to the sedately pedestrian Via Toledo. It was definitively *not* a *zona pedonale*. *Motociclette* roared up and down in both directions, jousting with mothers pushing baby carriages, folks on errands, old men—neither on crack nor on cell phones—actually talking to themselves, and young men balancing dozens of eggs on a bicycle's handlebars as though the whole scenario were being orchestrated by a mad choreographer. To top the parade, a young woman zipped by her, baby strapped in front, dog holding on behind. Lisa flattened her back against a wall to get her bearings. This was utter chaos! She loved it. Her nostrils flared. Her blood came alive. Let's see, what was it she needed to buy? She'd forgotten.

But instead of feeling panicked by her forgetfulness, she relaxed and started darting among the motor scooters as though she were running with the bulls at Pamplona. She would know what she needed when she spotted it. She picked up the rhythm, turning sideways when she heard buzzing behind her, sidestepping like a tap dancer when the *ciclisti* were coming directly at her. She focused on the faces of the women, men, and kids that were going about their business as casually as the strollers on Via Toledo below. Clearly they were oblivious to the hubbub, like beekeepers wearing hazmat suits collecting honey from a buzzing hive. She fell into their pattern and began dodging among the narrow streets and alleys of this Quartieri Spagnoli, as the maps she later consulted called it. It felt like her neighborhood in Brooklyn, only on happy steroids.

Her eyes shone with wonder at the fishmongers and their displays of tiny *vongole* (clams), succulent *cozze* (mussels), and shiny tiny *alici* (anchovies). Lisa loved seafood.

She found a supermarket with an entire wall of cheeses. She wanted to try them all. But what was the hurry? It was okay just to reconnoiter and let her feet take her where they willed.

She turned a corner into a small piazza and found herself facing a graceful staircase leading up to three stately *portici* that welcomed faithful to the Chiesa della Santissima Trinità degli Spagnoli, the church of the Most Holy Trinity of the Spaniards. She mounted the stairs and went in through the stained glass door.

The austere beauty of the interior was enhanced by the chanting of a priest, who faced a small congregation attending his evening Mass. She felt out of place, flashing back to those few occasions of marriage and funeral when she'd found herself again in the dreaded temple of her childhood and early adolescence.

But this is a beautiful place of peace. It's no threat to me.

It dawned on her that it was the *perfect* place for her to do her T.M., the twice-daily practice of meditation she'd signed up for after reading David Lynch's manuscript, *Catching the Big Fish*.

That had been another "dark day at the office," the marketing department babbling that the book's off-size shape and uneven chapters "didn't fit in" at the bookstore chains—and, besides, the author wasn't well-known enough. She'd even read them her favorite paragraph:

> In work and in life, we're all supposed to get along. We're supposed to have so much fun, like puppy dogs with our tails wagging. It's supposed to be great living; it's supposed to be fantastic.

But when she looked up from the page, nobody at the Standard table was smiling. The marketing folks' eyes were flat, impassive.

"European film critics voted his *Mulholland Drive* the best movie ever," she retorted. In vain. "We rest our case," they countered, "America is not Europe," closing the gateway on Mr. Lynch. She added the book to her list of dead soldiers, and to her growing agida with the profession she'd signed into.

She had developed a pattern of internalizing her rejections, incorporating something from their pages into her life. Which is what led her to start the daily meditation routine.

Today the prescribed twenty minutes went by as though in an instant, yet the transcendent feeling—from the mental exercise and the chanting of the small congregation—lingered after she left the church. She decided then and there that she would do at least one of her two daily sessions in a different church. She'd read that Naples was the "city of 1,200 churches." This way she could experience them without turning into a reverse lapsed Catholic. She would reserve her right to do her morning meditation in her rooftop paradise.

Walking down the steps of Santissima Trinità, travel fatigue fell upon her in earnest. Her limbs were turning to lead and she had to force herself to put one foot after another.

Lisa headed back in what she hoped was the direction in which she'd come, but was soon overwhelmed by a heavenly odor she surely would have remembered if she'd encountered it on the way up. She stopped in front of an ancient trattoria that straddled both sides of the tiny street. The waiter, whose thin figure belied his profession, was just setting a last table and chairs on the street. She looked around for *motociclette* but saw that this was another *zona pedonale*.

"*Già aperto?* Are you open yet?" she asked him.

"*Sì, pecché no?*" he shrugged, and gestured her to a straw-seated chair.

When she sank into it gratefully, she realized both the chair and the table were at crazy unnatural angles to the street, which turned them into comical leaning towers. Magically, the transparent blue glasses he laid on its cheerful checkered cloth stayed upright. Deciding to have a bite at her first Neapolitan restaurant before crashing made her feel wildly daring. She was hungry, having taken nothing since the drink on the train.

"*Niro, o janco?*" ("Red or white?") the waiter asked.

That much Napulitan' she remembered. "*Niro, pe ppiacere,*" she said, knowing her face was flushing as she said it.

"*Naturale o gassata?*"

She understood he was asking about water. "*Naturale, grazie,*" she answered. She remembered Babbino claiming fizzy water was "bad for the *deggestione*."

Within minutes the waiter returned with a bottle of flat mineral water. He added a wine glass and small carafe of red wine to the leaning array.

Lisa wasn't the least self-conscious about dining alone, something that sometimes spooked her in New York. The *vino niro* was hearty, refreshing, filled with life. Her energy flowed back and, with it, even greater appetite. She glanced at the simple card he'd handed her. It listed five or six pizzas, but she read why this was more than enough. The place, called "Brandi, Antica Pizzeria della Regina d'Italia," was established in 1780—"six years before the U.S. even had a Constitution." The owner of this very restaurant, back in the nineteenth century, had invented Pizza Margherita because its ingredients—basil, tomatoes, crushed garlic cloves, and mozzarella to match the colors of the Italian flag—were Queen Margherita's favorite topping.

The aroma that guided Lisa's feet here was exactly what the waiter served her. It looked good enough to devour in a single bite. Her hands were trembling as she cut into it. She was famished.

After disposing of the first two slices, she forced herself to slow down to savor simply the best pizza she'd ever tasted. Like most New Yorkers, she revered a good pizza, and had her fervent preferences; but her previous history with pizza was out the window at first bite. It was as though she'd been led from a cave and was, for the first time, seeing the light. The ingredients were so fresh she could taste the earth they issued from, and the crust was crusty and flaky, and at the same time soft enough to dissolve in your mouth.

"*Tutte bo'?*" the waiter inquired.

"*Si, assaj' bon.*" The phrase was how everyone in her family responded to Babbino's sauces.

The waiter eyed her carafe. "*Po cchiù vino?*" he asked.

She nodded. *"Pecche no?"* she answered, as though she were a native.

The waiter gave her a smile, as if he read her mind, knew she was struggling with the language but approving her earnestness.

She would ask him about the wine when he returned. She looked from the table to the full moon lighting up the air and wished she had someone to share the moment with.

As though in answer to her passing thought, a man who looked slightly Asian walked up Salita di S. Anna, singing a folk song. Though he must have been her age or not much older, his voice was as resonant and sonorous as this splendid evening's atmosphere. He caught her eye, fell silent, and then segued into a lilting melodic quaver: *"O sole mio!"*

Hearing the universally known Neapolitan folk song directed at her gave Lisa goosebumps. The stranger carried the famous tune quite well. No wonder a small band of listeners followed along behind him.

The neighborhood had become even more crowded than an hour ago, now that the sun was setting and the evening was moving into first gear. Among the crowd of listeners behind the singing stranger were twin sisters, dressed identically, linking arms as they walked along the narrow street. For a moment she was disconcerted. *He's walking along happy-go-lucky with a song on his lips. I'm just sitting here like a bump on a log.* The moment passed, but as she noticed the gooseflesh again she recalled what the dapper stranger in Brooklyn told Sammie to tell her. "When you first feel the magic…" I don't even *have* a rosary, she thought.

The new carafe appeared before her as if by the same magic. She met the waiter's glance as he picked up the empty one. Her glance confirmed that she *loved* this wine.

"*Come si chiama questo vino?*" ("What is this wine called?") she asked, reverting to classroom Italian.

If he understood, or even heard, her, the waiter didn't show it. But a moment later, he returned from the kitchen carrying the bottle.

She took the bottle from him. It *was* a night of miracles. The label read *"Greco di Tufo."*

"*Il mio nome!*" she exclaimed.

His frown was priceless.

"*Mi chiamo Lisa* Greco" ("My name is Lisa Greco") she said, shaking his hand.

His laugh was response enough. "*Allora, brava!*" he saluted her, "*Il vin' è sulla cas'.*" Then he added, *"Io, mi chiam' Riccardo."*

She was pretty sure Riccardo was telling her that her wine was on the house.

Now he was removing the dishes, hers perfectly cleaned, and looked at her as though to say, "Was there something wrong with the *plate*?" Clearly she had room for more. "*Vorrebb' altro?*" he asked. "Would you like something else?"

She didn't feel like anything sweet. Her tongue was too happy with new discoveries to want to numb itself with sugar. Lisa's brow wrinkled as she pondered Riccardo's question. "Maybe a taste of seafood," she mumbled without realizing she was speaking aloud.

Riccardo nodded, his expression unchanging, and disappeared again into the kitchen. He returned a few moments later bearing an oval plate filled with the smallest clams she'd ever seen, in a clear light broth, flavored with garlic, lemon, and—was it?—shallots. Omigod—she savored the first bites. *I've never tasted anything this good in my life. It was the perfect dessert.*

When she finally stood up to leave, steadying herself to adjust to the cobblestones after her slanted meal, Riccardo came out to bid her off.

"*Venga torna subito,*" he said, saluting again. "Come back soon."

She made her way back to Via Toledo numb with exhaustion but stuffed and happy. Along the way, half-consciously, she picked up a container of cream, a very ripe persimmon, four eggs the grocer wrapped in newspaper, and a large bottle of mineral water—*naturale.*

She wouldn't remember the little elevator, the flight of stairs, the courtyard, or letting herself into her flat. She would just recall how perfect the bed felt as she tumbled into it and, without removing her clothes or closing the French doors, consigned herself to dreamless sleep.

Eleven

LISA AWOKE TO THE SOUNDS and smells of rain, the low grumbling of thunder as though the sky above were sniffing hungry at the open doors to her tiny balcony. She smiled. Unlike the angry assault of the biting cold rain she lived with in Brooklyn, this rain was warm, friendly, almost laughing. She let it fill her senses as she lay cuddled in the thin blanket. She took deep breaths until she could figure out what was different this morning. She felt no hollowness, like the hollowness that set in inevitably when it was raining in New York and her life was twisting in the wind, drifting from one reaction to the next, without direction, without heart, without hope. She always felt as though she were missing something, and that being in the rain while missing something, while not even knowing what she was missing, was dreadfully wrong.

But in this morning's rain, she felt nothing but sweet elation, or some feeling she couldn't identify that was sweet. Was it content? She felt unthreatened, at peace with herself.

Maybe what she was missing all along was *being here*.

She smiled again as that exuberant aria ran through her head. *"Funiculì, funiculà."* Lisa breathed in the uniqueness of it all, settled back into her pillows, closed her eyes, and slept another hour.

She didn't need to be anywhere.

This time the sun awakened her. She stretched, then jumped out of bed and into the bathroom to wash her face.

She was hungry again. Couldn't wait to get outside where, already, she could hear singing in the street. She felt like a little girl on Christmas morning before Christmas morning became an adult's disappointment.

On the street side of the big green door, she saw that the old tenor was back in yesterday's position, cheering the crowd with a heartfelt tune that she didn't recognize but that was making his listeners laugh out loud. What are those words? She couldn't quite make them out, but they sounded like *pure li pisce nce fanno a ll'ammore*— even the fish make love? Was that *Napulitan'* too? Lisa smiled as she took a chair beneath the canvas that covered the wire tables of the tiny café in the square.

A waiter materialized to take her order for a double espresso macchiato, asked her if she wanted *"caccusarella altr'"* ("some little thing else"). When she nodded enthusiastically, he gestured for her to stand up and follow him. Inside she saw why: the long glass counter was filled with *doce* and *panini* (sweets and little sandwiches). The panorama of temptation made her stomach rumble. She settled for a delicately wedged ham and cheese *crostino* that satisfied her newly-awakened appetite for sweet and substantial.

The crostino was unbelievably fresh, beyond scrumptious. She finished it just as her second *duppio macchiato* arrived to buy her time to plan this morning's mission. She would do her morning meditation at one of the cathedrals Naples was world-famous for, and if a gift shop offered itself there, maybe she'd look for a rosary. She remembered her grandfather's wooden beads that he used every day to recite "Hail Marys" in tandem with the daily Vatican broadcast led by "our Holy Father in Rome." If only he'd left the rosary to me instead of the cufflinks, Lisa thought. With his cufflinks gone, she no longer had anything tangible to connect her with the only ancestor she'd known well. She kicked herself for not showing Fabio the gold pendant to see if he could identify it, but tucked away from sight it had been out of mind.

San Gennaro, she remembered. The saint Babbino had told her about, whose blood liquefied every year on his feast day. On the few occasions when that miracle *does not* happen, he told her, Naples would face certain disaster. Babbino had told her so many stories she couldn't remember half of them but this one stood out as typically Catholic and particularly creepy. She googled walking directions to her destination. The sainted bishop's blood was enshrined on Via Duomo, in the metropolitan cathedral, episcopal seat of the archdiocese of Naples.

On the map it looked a long ways, but Google said twenty minutes and it was correct. Lisa thought how different history might be if Marco Polo or Christopher Columbus had GPS. In today's world everything was already known, mapped, and photographed from space. What could be left to discover?

She walked straight down Via Toledo to Via Armando Diaz, where she turned right and walked toward Corso Umberto. On her left, she passed a Fascist-era building that caught her eye. Its architecture included a wide apron on the side facing her. The apron was crowded with couples—of every possible gender combination she knew of and some, she guessed, that she did not know—wrapped in each other's arms. She automatically turned her eyes away, though she also noticed that none of them seemed to mind that passersby were staring. The idea of many couples kissing in the open—a gathering of lovers—seemed immensely happy. She smiled at them. They smiled back.

On a whim she wandered away from her googled route, taking a wide alley with a stone arch at the end. Beyond the arch she found herself in Piazza Dante Alighieri, where a statue of the greatest Italian poet, whose eloquently precise Tuscan shaped today's standard Italian, dominated the large plaza that hosted Burger King, an "R-Store" bearing the Apple logo, and the ancient gate to the Città Vecchia, the Old City.

Passing through the gate she was astonished to find several blocks of bookstores, one after another—more than a New York bookseller could imagine in her wildest dreams. I guess they didn't get the memo that bookstores were fading away, she thought. She followed the endless stores through the streets of the ancient University of Naples. Trattorias and bars and lodgings were named after Bellini, Sannazaro, Rossini, Verdi, Tasso, Boccaccio—so many names of Naples' famous composers and writers that her mind reeled as she walked past them, reliving happy hours at Yale lost in the worlds they created.

When she turned onto Via Duomo, the Catedrale di Santa Maria Assunta, nicknamed "San Gennaro," greeted her—an unlikely amalgam of nearly every architectural style she'd studied, from French Gothic to Renaissance to Baroque to Neo-Gothic. But it somehow made its point: stately, grand, demanding respect. A plaque said its construction began in the thirteenth century and wasn't completed until the twentieth—700 years in the making. The bruised red Renaissance villa that abutted the church on its left relieved the eye with its relative purity.

Then she did a proverbial double take. Gooseflesh formed on her arms again.

The same Asian-looking man who'd caught her ear last night when he strolled by her table was at this moment entering the corner shop, *Mastranza Arredi Sacri*—an ecclesiastical store. She allowed her feet to turn toward the shop instead of toward the cathedral's entrance for its display windows were filled with rosaries as well as vestments and priestly attire.

She entered to the tinkling of a bell, and sure enough, the man with jet-black hair turned to face her. She could see a flicker of recognition in his eyes. But, not to be rude, he quickly looked back to the bald-headed clerk to explain what he was shopping for. Lisa watched the clerk hand the singing stranger a black vest-like piece of clothing topped with a roman color. The singer's a priest, for chrissakes. Wouldn't you know it?

She turned away to leave the shop and head for the cathedral. But before she reached the door Lisa whirled on her heels and returned to her former mission. What in the world is wrong with me? The man, priest or not, is a complete stranger. Why should I *not* stay here?

The inside of the stuffy shop was dim, and it took a few more moments for her eyes to fully adjust from the bright Neapolitan sun. The singer-priest was handing back the black shirt and pointing to another row of collars. The shop clerk stood on tiptoe to grab the one he was pointing to—one attached to a black serge vest that was ribbed with violet. The singer's fingers caressed the ribbing slowly, before a smile illuminated his face. "*'Sto è quall' che vulé*" ("This is the one I want") he pronounced with a playful lilt in his voice. The clerk watched him stand in front of the mirror to try the vest and collar on, as though this were his first priestly purchase. He couldn't be a bishop, could he? She couldn't remember what the various colors signified.

Lisa scanned the shop for the rosaries. There they were—an entire wall of them. Arranged in order from black to white, dark to light, with every color of the liturgical rainbow in between. She scanned them until she saw the several rows of brown. Sure enough, a few of the brown rosaries seemed to be made of wood. She approached them skeptically, but when she reached out her hand to touch, they were indeed wood. Just like her grandfather's. It didn't take her long to choose one. The old clerk saw she'd made a decision and approached her. "*Vuole questa?*" he asked. "*Sì,*" she answered, "*per piacere.*"

"*È fatto di legno d'ulivo,*" ("It's made of olive wood") the clerk said.

Meanwhile the collared stranger was watching her intently, the spark of recognition growing in his eyes. She stared back at him boldly. After all, he was just a cleric. He smiled. Lisa smiled back, gooseflesh returning to her arm. His eyes were so intense. But she busied herself making payment, and retreated from the shop. Why was her heart pounding?

Inside the metropolitan cathedral, she stood in awe of the sheer beauty of the stained glass behind the main altar. The busts of every bishop of Naples from Asprenas to Michele Giordano presided along the main aisle where Stations of the Cross normally were. Remembering her daily discipline, she found her way to the side altar dedicated to *San Gennaro*, Saint January, the city's patron saint. A fellow Capricorn. She settled into a wooden pew.

She removed the new rosary from the little velvet pouch and ran her fingers across the smooth, irregularly shaped beads. Fingering them like a pious Catholic, she closed her eyes and took in the silence of this immense structure dedicated to an outdated God with whom she'd always had an arm's-length relationship with at best. She began her meditation by thanking Babbino for bringing her here.

And also thanking Sammie's Dapper Man.

Her twenty minutes passed so quickly she had to look twice when she opened her eyes to check her phone's stop watch. This meditation was so powerful it took her by surprise. She felt she'd just excavated her way to a whole new undiscovered basement of her mind, opening its door to sheer and intense color. The feeling of joy came over her again, mixed this time with peace—and happy anticipation of her next session. For the first time she could remember, she felt grounded.

Her stomach grumbled leaving the church. She crossed to the tabacchi across the street and ordered a macchiato and one of the enticingly exquisite pastries that smelt like it had just exited a nearby oven.

Taking a chair on the street she watched the passersby. She loved that the men were wearing colorful trousers and jackets, some smoking pipes. She loved their tri-colored eyeglasses, with stems and lens frames yellow, red, and green. She wondered about the Asian singer-priest again. He *was* pretty danged handsome. She closed her eyes and fantasized about sitting on the ledge of that building on Via Armando Diaz, making out with him among all the other couples.

What was getting into her? Her blood rushed to her skin so strongly she could feel it. She closed her eyes to restore control.

Twelve

"ARE YOU OKAY? *DAIJOUBU DES'KA?*" a male voice said.

When Lisa opened her eyes, she nearly choked.

It was the singing stranger in his new collar, standing in front of her and looking at her intensely as though he were a medical missionary assessing a wounded native.

"I'm fine," she stammered, knowing her blood was racing even more. "The espresso just gave me a rush."

He stood there, waiting for something more. "We've got stop meeting like this," he finally said with a smile.

So he did recognize her. "You walked by my table last night singing 'O Sole mio.'"

This time he looked slightly embarrassed. "I guess seeing pretty woman naturally makes me burst into song. May I join you?"

She didn't know quite what to say.

He took her silence as invitation and set his package on her table's empty seat. "I'll just get *kohi*. Would you like another?"

"I'm not sure I should dare, father," she answered lamely. "Maybe a water."

He nodded, and looked like he was going to say something but thought better of it. He ducked into the shop—then immediately popped back out. "Don't call me father," he said, his eyes twinkling. "My name is Ichiro." Then went back into the tabacchi.

Which gave her time to collect her wits, and review what had just happened. But the effort was futile. Had she insulted him? Did he have a higher title than "father"? She had no idea. His accent *was* charming though. She'd heard once that Japanese had no articles and very few prepositions. Simple and direct.

This was Naples, not Manhattan. So who cared? She would go with the flow and see where today's zigzagging was leading her.

The stranger came back with his espresso and set a water in front of her.

"How long have you been in Naples?" he asked.

"This is my first morning. I got here last night."

"So last night was first meal here?"

She nodded. "Yes."

"Sorry to eat alone."

Her voice was firm. "I'm *fine* being alone," she said, sounding every bit like the New Haven feminist she never was.

"So am I—*hontoni*, really," he said unexpectedly. "Solitude is a great blessing. How many times you come here?"

She shook her head. "This is my first."

His dark eyes gave her a fuller inspection, as though calculating how an attractive young woman could find herself alone in this of all cities. "What do you think?"

His questions were so innocent and direct she couldn't resist. Her response was whole-hearted. "I *love* it," she said. "What about you?"

"I like it very much," he said. "I come from Tokyo every year. Napoli my second home. My father was born here."

Her eyes widened. So he was half-Japanese, half-Italian. That certainly explained his rugged handsomeness, and mysterious eyes. "You must know Napoli well."

"As well as anyone can know this most enigmatic of all cities."

"What brings you here so often?" she asked.

He started to answer, but thought better of it. "What are dinner plans tonight?"

The question was as abrupt as it was bold.

"I have no plans yet. I'm just following my nose. That's one of the reasons I needed to come here," she answered.

"*Segoi des'*," he said. "*Buonissimo* ("Excellent"). Then you must come find out for yourself."

"Find out what?"

"What brings me back to Napoli."

Thirteen

SHE COULDN'T BELIEVE SHE WAS doing this. The singing priest or whoever he was had handed her a restaurant card, then stood up and left. His parting line: "Come after eight. You are my guest." She opened her mouth to protest, but it was too late. He'd already disappeared around the corner. When she stood up to walk after him, she was swimming upstream against a tide of ribald German soccer players. The priest, Bishop or Monsignor Ichiro or whatever, was nowhere in sight. He'd left her with a million questions. Was he really Japanese? What in the world had she agreed to?

Back in her rooftop flat, she laughed out loud to think of it. After all, there was no harm done. She had no intention of going to a night-time rendezvous with a perfect stranger, priest or not.

She poured herself a small glass of peppery Aglianico, and slurped down half the persimmon with a spoon—it tasted like an exquisite gelato. Then she positioned herself on the big terrace overlooking the stately glass and steel cupola, opened her notebook, and started typing furiously. By the time Lisa looked up it was two hours later. The sun had long since set, and she hadn't even noticed. She was lost in her work. What she was writing was turning into a narrative, the backbone of a story! It hadn't started that way. It had started with wandering all over the page, a random odyssey whose hero was trying to figure out what home it was that she was returning to. Searching for a clue. Searching for the meaning of a gold pendant. A shape was beginning to manifest itself, one that excited her. Beneath it all, like subtext, was her wondering if she was truly creative, or just wanting to *prove* herself. To the world? No! To herself.

She looked away from the screen for a moment, then checked her watch.

It was seven-thirty.

She stood up, stretched, and cocked her head to hear lines of song wafting up from the street:

Quanno sponta la luna a Marechiare
pure li pisce nce fanno a ll'amore.

She grabbed her new scarf and the business card and, a lilt in her step, walked out the door humming the cheerful tune.

Fourteen

WHEN LISA GRECO WAS IN high school, she'd read a red-covered paperback copy of Kurt Vonnegut's zany novel *Cat's Cradle* and ran across a statement from the comic, cynical Jamaican prophet named "Bokonon": "*Peculiar travel directions are dancing lessons from God.*" Vonnegut became her favorite author though he'd never make it through an acquisitions committee today. She'd never forgotten the line, though she'd rarely applied it much either. In her busy Manhattan life, she was known for turning down invitations to the Jersey shore, Fire Island, New England to see the leaves at their prime. There was just too much work to do first.

But this time would be different. This was going to be her time. She would do the unexpected. Heading seaward on Via Toledo, Vonnegut's line kept repeating itself like an insistent jingle. On this trip, she would obey the crackpot prophet. Bokonon's observation resonated with her soul—the soul that had been frozen in New York winter now awakened by this warm and happy city filled with heavenly sounds and scents. What could be more fortuitous than accepting the mysterious travel directions from the mysterious priestly stranger?

To her consternation she arrived at the address on the card, Piazza Santa Maria La Nova, 17, exactly at eight. The green awning bore the name "Ristorante A'Canzuncella," confirming she was in the right place. Being prompt had always been one of her social vices.

The restaurant was in a dimly-lit cul-de-sac flanking a red-tile-roofed cathedral that appeared to be shuttered. Well, he *is* some kind of priest after all. Maybe he's just gotten off work?

Lisa saw a human pod of what must be workers smoking by the front door. She wasn't sure whether to go in or not, but finally drew bravery from her purple scarf and marched to the door. They all looked at her with what she swore was puzzlement as she went in.

Immediately she could see why they looked baffled: the down staircase gave her a view of the entire restaurant—a cozy, vaulted cave, tables nicely set for dinner, but with no sign of diners. She was too early!

No way to conceal she was a tourist through and through, she took the steps slowly. When she'd reached the main floor, a dignified middle-aged woman with close-cropped orange-blonde curls walked out of the kitchen to greet her. She didn't look quite as startled as the guys outside the door. Maybe she was used to Americans.

"*Ha prenotato?* ("Do you have reservations?") the woman asked.

Lisa didn't know how to respond. Then she remembered. "*Sono…un ospite di Ichiro*" ("I'm a guest of Ichiro").

The woman's facial expression changed immediately to a big smile. She beckoned Lisa to follow. She led her to the first table for two facing what seemed to be a small performance stage, with a piano to one side and a slightly raised bandstand on the other. Lisa sat down self-consciously. "Am I the only one here?" she asked. "He told me to meet him at eight."

The woman laughed a deep-throated laugh. "Oh, no," she reassured her. "Many people come. *Janco o russo?*" the red-haired woman asked.

"*Russo, per piacere,*" Lisa answered.

As Lisa looked around the arched brick walls, the woman went off to find the wine. The alcove across from her table was frescoed with twin-peaked Vesuvius presiding over the Bay of Naples. Other walls were adorned with musical motifs. When the woman returned with a carafe of red wine, she wanted to ask her about Ichiro but restrained herself. What difference did it make? She didn't have a train to catch or a marketing meeting to attend. She was relaxing, here to soak in the city of her family origins, to find out more about her past, in order to find out more about herself—and maybe her future.

She sipped the wine and continued checking the place out. The cheerful tables were uniformly decked with bright yellow paper tablecloths dressed with vintage records—78s for placemats, 45s for coasters. She saw that the 45 now bearing her wine glass was Louie Armstrong's "Ain't Misbehavin'" and moved her plate enough to reveal that the 78 it rested on was Enrico Caruso's "For You Alone." Its red label showed a dog looking into an antique Victrola. All the tables were set with old records. I like this place already, she thought. It's original.

At eight-twenty she excused herself to no one, and headed for the ladies' room. Unlike her girlfriends in New York, who never went to the bathroom without asking someone where it was, she headed directly for the back of the room. Where else could it be?

The blue door to the *servizi,* marked with a male and female stick

figure, was up a short flight of red brick stairs on the far wall. Lisa opened it—and almost fainted.

In the dim light a creature wearing black and pink silk robes sat facing her. He had a devilish white mask with an enormous nose and darkened eyes, and a multi-flopped crown. The white-face looked both sad and sinister at the same time. Overwhelmed by a surge of claustrophobia, Lisa beat her retreat back through the blue door to her table. She didn't need to wash her face *that* badly.

She was spooked, and took a calming sip of wine.

The woman returned and seemed to look at her knowingly. But she was bearing a plate of delicate seafood: sashimi-like slices of tuna, surrounded with the tiny *alici* fish she would later identify as anchovies—served on a bed of lemon slices and fresh Italian parsley.

Lisa realized she was hungry. She picked up her fork, put it back down, and asked the woman, "Are you sure Ichiro is coming?"

The woman understood the hesitation in her voice. "*Sì, sì,*" she answered. "He is here. He will eat later." Her abrupt departure underlined the authority of her instructions. But they made no sense to Lisa. What was going on? *Pacienza,* she scolded herself, remembering her Babbino's chiding. Patience had never been her forte. But the word in Neapolitan was somehow more embraceable. "Dancing lessons," she reminded herself.

These baby anchovies were beyond delicious, not at all like the over-salted anchovies used on pizza. They were naturally sweet and lightly bathed in white vinegar, whetting her appetite perfectly. She took her time enjoying them, salivating at each citrusy bite.

Suddenly she didn't mind being the only one in the place. She felt regal, like Queen Margherita in her Savoian palace. Dancing lessons.

It was not until nearly nine o'clock that other diners began arriving as though by strict rules of etiquette: parties of two, and three, and more—one group of ten—whose origins she guessed as each party descended the entry staircase. The greeting woman—was she the owner? —gave way to one of the waiters she'd noticed smoking at the door. But now he was wearing a formal maroon jacket and was all business as he removed her empty plate and handed her a menu.

Though it wasn't exactly a menu. Just a list of the courses—seven in all. I guess the fish plate didn't count. Her head reeled as she read through them: *polpettini con basilico ed aceto* (baby octopus with basil and vinegar), *frittura mista di pesci* (mixed fried fish), *bruschette con seppioline* (bruschetta with baby squid)—and this was just appetizers. I can never eat all this. She stared at empty plate across from her and wondered if Ichiro was trying to kill her before he even showed up.

But her stalwart Italian blood came to her rescue, and she reminded herself she'd eaten hardly anything all day.

The music began at nine-thirty. The orange-haired greeting lady who served her originally turned out to be a full-voiced prima donna. She belted out a Neapolitan folk song that made the dining room, already a little tipsy, ring freely with raucous happiness. The woman was accompanied by a guitarist with shaggy black hair and a smile so welcoming it made his missing teeth look grand.

When the folk songs ended, the proprietress made an announcement. She asked for a big hand for the next singer, "a man from very far away who loves our city so much he comes back every year to thrill us with his *voce clara*. Please welcome Ichiro Negroponte."

Sure enough, it was her Monsignor Ichiro who issued from the kitchen, wearing his new Roman collar, a short-sleeved dress shirt with a pen in its pocket, and pink trousers. The pen is an odd touch, she thought. His hair was slicked back in the style of old-time tenors, his eyes more Asian than Italian, and his dangerous smile aimed directly at her. He was even handsomer than she remembered.

Lisa's gooseflesh returned. It was the magic, announcing itself again.

Ichiro took the mike from the lady and broke into Puccini's *Nessun dorma*. By the time he reached "*Vincero! Vincero!*" there wasn't a dry eye in the room. Lisa wiped away tears and gave him her warmest smile. Why did he have to be a goddam priest!?

The next half hour passed like a dream as, one after another, Ichiro did convincing tribute to *Funiculì, Funiculà, Santa Lucia,* and *Torna a Surriento*—breaking hearts table by table: Neapolitan, Milanese, Chinese, Roman, French, German—and American.

Halfway through his performance that had enlisted the enthusiastic applause of the whole audience, the rhythmic clapping slowed and stopped. No one wanted to miss or interrupt a single note issuing from this mouth.

When Ichiro finished and took a modest bow, all sprang to their feet with shouts of Bravo!

Lisa was shouting, too. "Encore, encore!"

He directed a gallant bow her way, graciously extending his arms to signal the guitarist. She didn't recognize the opening words— *Partirono le rondini dal mio paese freddo e senza sole* (The swallows have departed from my cold country with no sun) —though the melody struck a chord deep within her. But as the song rose to a close, echoing from Ichiro's heart to hers, Lisa recalled the words from her childhood when Babbino would break into song at unexpected moments:

> *Non ti scordar di me*
> *La vita mia legata a te*
> *Io t'amo sempre più*

Nel sogno mio rimani tu
Non ti scordar di me

It was another of those melodies that haunted her, and she could never forget the first time she'd heard the words in English. It happened the day that started with her first plane flight ever.

Ichiro was blowing her a kiss, then took another bow, and headed for her table. Sweat poured down his forehead and he reached with his handkerchief to deal with it. Then he noticed her tears.

Lisa was making a feeble attempt to stop them from bathing her face entirely, finally reaching for the second clean handkerchief he retrieved and was handing her. Thank God she wasn't wearing makeup. "I'm sorry," she said, taking control of her voice to explain that day when, just arrived in Buffalo from her first plane ride she watched a cousin—one who bullied her on those rare occasions they saw each other—make his way to the pulpit at her Babbino's funeral. There he belted out the words to the familiar melody:

> Don't forget about me:
> My life is bound to you
> I love you more and more
> You live in my dreams
> Don't forget about me
> My life is bound to you
> A nest awaits you
> In my heart
> Don't forget about me
> Don't forget about me!

Now her eyes were wet again. "He was the only one in my family who really loved me—and who I truly loved," she said.

"What was your cousin's name?"

She gave him a look. "My cousin? I *loathed* my cousin. I wondered how someone so nasty could have such a beautiful voice. No, it's my grandfather I loved. And the words never left my mind. 'Don't forget about me…My life is bound to you…A nest awaits you in my heart.'" She took a deep breath and allowed herself a few more tears.

Ichiro reached for her hand across the table, held it firmly in his until she was done.

His touch electrified her. "I guess music can be powerful," she finally said.

He nodded solemnly. "It can be exhausting."

When he took his hand away, Lisa missed its warmth. Then her eyes widened. He was unsnapping the Roman collar and removing it. Her brow wrinkled her question: "What are you doing?"

He folded the collar and hung it on his chair behind him, then wiped his brow again. "I'm having dinner with you. I'm famished."

"What about your collar?" she asked.

"My collar has served purpose. I always wear one kind of collar or another when I perform," he answered, admiring the plate of fish the waiter placed in front of him. "It draws attention away from my eyes," he joked. "Actually, it helps me feel the confidence. Otherwise I can be tongue-tied. Last week I wore King of Naples' ruffle."

"It's your powerful voice that holds our attention," she said. "And there's nothing wrong with your eyes either."

He put his hands together, briefly, and bowed. *"Itadakimas,"* he said, and picked up his fork.

The phrase was familiar. Her Japanese-American editor-friend at Standard, Yuki Mitsumatsu, never began a meal without the ritual invocation that showed gratitude. Lisa filled Ichiro's glass from the carafe.

"Are you telling me you're not a priest?"

"Dio mio, no," he said. "I'm a professor of theoretical mathematics at Jesuit University in Tokyo. A practicing Buddhist. And

apprentice tenor here. Please forgive my weak performance." He reached into his pocket, and handed her his card.

"There was nothing weak about your performance," she protested. She examined his card. Ichiro Negroponte was "Professor of Algebraic Topology" at Sophia. "I don't know what to say. I was terrible at algebra," she confessed.

Ichiro laughed. "No need to say—just enjoy. You're my guest. I will not examine your algebra." He raised his glass for a toast. "*Salute!*"

Grateful for the time to collect her wits, she raised hers. "*Bravo, maestro! Salute!*"

They clinked glasses.

"You're not hungry?" Ichiro asked her, noticing her fork at rest.

She shook her head, and blurted it out: "*Mo kekkou desu*"—another phrase Yuki used. "Not anymore." It feels like I've been eating for hours," she replied. "Everything's so good."

He gave her an intrigued look. "You speak Japanese?"

"Not at all," she assured him.

But she, too, was intrigued—by this man whose experience stretched from the austerity of mathematics to the robust rigors of opera.

He was telling her that the connection between math and music was profound and ancient. One of the earliest Greek philosophers, Pythagoras, believed that the universe itself was generated from numbers. He was the first to leave writings about the "harmony of the spheres"—or the "music of the spheres." It's the theory that each galaxy, star, moon, and planet reverberated with its own unique sound that was determined mathematically by its bulk, speed, and orbit. "The result is a cosmic symphony that never ends. We're actually bathed in music all the time," he proclaimed. "Every moon, from Uranus' Miranda to Saturn's Titan to our own, broadcasts its own distinctive chords. The universe is a mathematical puzzle inviting our involvement."

"And admiration," she added. As his fervor magnified, she encouraged him to tell her more.

He continued between bites. "Today astronomical audio scopes monitor this music from space. Computer science is working on programs that translate it mathematically. We are identifying the tonal equations that govern all celestial motion."

His excitement was compelling. She couldn't believe that the girl from Buffalo who barely understood "a word" of algebra, geometry, and physics was being mesmerized by an opera singing wannabe who was able to describe the music of the spheres as clearly as he strove to master the bel canto of Rossini.

"What will you *do* with these passions?" she asked. Sheesh, I sound like my mother's reaction to my declaring an English major at Yale. "I mean..." She wanted him to know she wasn't being critical, "How do you put this all together?"

"You mean in my career, or in my mind and spirit?" He laughed. "I wish Japanese could be as direct as Americans and Italians."

"I'm sorry. Am I being too personal?"

"I like it very much. You have no idea what it's like living in a culture that struggles to give voice to *anything* other than expressions of politeness. I feel free when I'm here. Conversing like this is really liberating."

"I'm just wondering which you're most serious about, deep down. Math or singing?"

He didn't hesitate. "Both. Answer to your question is that I have no clear idea how this double pursuit will turn out. One of life's greatest gifts is that we can't see the future. I only know, with absolute certainty, that what I do feels natural to me, like it's my nature." His half-joking tone turned serious. "So naturally I must continue it

71

until…" His voice trailed off, as the self-consciousness of his Japanese mother took hold.

"Until?" She wasn't going to let him pull back.

"Until something decisive happens," he said. He looked into her eyes.

She turned her eyes away. She was feeling pinned to a corkboard, like a butterfly that hadn't yet flown enough to be arrested in flight by an outside force. That, after all, was why she had to take a break from her life in New York. She wasn't ready to be pinned to anything not of her own choosing. "Listen," she said, breaking the silence. She hummed a few bars of the street song that had made the old singer's impromptu audiences laugh. "Do you know it?"

Abandoning his plate and fork, Ichiro sprang to his feet and approached the guitarist. "*Marechiare, pe ppiacere,*" he said. But the guitarist was already strumming the introductory chords, breaking into the folk song so effortlessly that diners who knew it just as immediately started to clap time:

> *Quanno spónta la luna a Marechiaro,*
> *Pure li pisce nce fanno a ll'ammore.,*
> *Se revòtano ll'onne de lu mare,*
> *Pe' la priézza cágnano culore.*
> *Quanno spónta la luna a Marechiaro!*

The laughing faces of the clappers confirmed that Lisa wasn't the only one delighted by the song.

"Bravo!" she said again as he bowed and sat back down across from her. "I've got to find the words in English."

Fifteen

THE REST OF THE EVENING passed in an enchanting blur. Between sets, Ichiro sat with her, shoveling huge portions of food into his mouth as though his life depended on it. Her eyes widened at the swaths he was cutting in the plates bearing the multiple courses. "Singing makes me ravenous." he said.

"More than theoretical mathematics?" she teased.

He made the wavy Italian hand gesture for things being equivalent.

"Seems like everything in Naples makes me hungry, too," she said. If she continued at this rate, she would gain ten pounds. "I guess I'm worried that this spectacular food will disappear before I've had my fill."

"I can assure it won't," he said, between bites. "It's always here. And it gets better." He drank as lustily as he ate.

She assaulted him with one question after another, until she'd learned that he first heard the dignified proprietress—her name was Donna Isolata—singing on the wide Harajuku Boulevard in Shibuya, and had come back to listen to her every day until she smiled in welcome and invited him to sit at her feet. All day, dripping heat or not, he would soak in the most thrilling music he'd ever known. As an aspiring topologist he couldn't help listening for the rhythmic space between notes, and the exuberant melodic surfaces uniquely created by her voice. At the end of the first summer—he was only seventeen at the time—Donna Isolata told him it was time for her to go back to Napoli, but that he should find his way there and learn to sing. "You love it so much," she told him, "you *must* do it."

Shortly before his nineteenth birthday Ichiro received his PhD after submitting a two-page thesis entitled "E.F. Lusk's Homeomorphic Embedding in Topological Spheres: A Challenge," and passing his oral exam with colors so flying that his "defense" was more or less a job interview for the university's only open assistant professor position. Then he moved parental mountains to make his first trip to Naples during the next school break. He looked up Donna Isolata. She took it in stride, more pleased than surprised that he'd found his way from the distant Orient to learn to sing. She gave him private lessons at first, in exchange for his performing in her restaurant. One year, when he was twenty-one, she declared that he'd outgrown her lessons and was ready to study at a conservatory—with a *maestro* who could mete out discipline like a karate master.

"That's exactly what young men need," his maestro insisted. Ichiro's life was filled with joy on the day he walked into the classroom presided over by Benvenuto Rizzardi—the same classroom in which Bellini and Verdi had studied. His first goal was to turn the eternal frown on maestro's face to a smile of hope.

Ichiro continued to return to Naples every summer, earning his way by a grant, by teaching Japanese as a second language and tutoring Scuola Superiore math students in topology. All the while he learned voice and measure and practiced the repertoire.

"How in the world did you talk your father into letting you go?"

He looked at her with glee in his dark eyes. "Simply, I was nineteen, with an advanced degree and a real job in my field, unheard for young person in Japan. No one could have stopped me. Besides, my father was Italian, remember?" He said it as though that were the only explanation necessary. "He was happy I wanted to learn more about the homeland he loved."

"What does your father do?"

Ichiro laughed. "In the empire of sushi, ramen, and soba, he opened one of the first Italian restaurants in Shibuya. I slaved in his kitchen until I headed off to college at fifteen."

"You were a precocious genius, were you?"

Ichiro smiled. "I thought of it as escape."

"It sounds like your father was allowing you to do what he wasn't able to do himself."

He nodded. She was precisely right. By the time Ichiro was thirteen, he had three younger siblings and his father and mother both had to work around the clock to support them. "He always said he would return here before he died." Ichiro paused. "He never did. I only hope that his spirit made its way here, and that's what I feel when I'm singing. His courage was my inspiration."

"Well, it's obvious your singing is inspired," she said. "Thank you for inviting me to hear it."

"I'm honored that you accepted my invitation." He raised his glass to her.

"What happened to your theoretical mathematics?"

"Are you checking up on me for my father?" he laughed. He reached into his back pocket, and unfolded a small sheaf of papers. "My most recent publication," he said, handing it to her with a modest grin. "Just came out."

Her eyes glanced down. It was an offprint from this month's *Geometry and Topology,* an academic journal. "I doubt I'll understand it," she said.

He watched her eyes as she took it in:

Hilbert Curves, Lindenmayer Systems, and Archimedes' Pilgrimage to the Labyrinth at Baia
By Ichiro Negroponte, PhD

We are familiar with the Hilbert Curve's capacity for filling an unlimited space with a single line doubling upon itself infinitely, and the time-management work-around of using Lindenmayer Systems, or L-Systems, to recreate the curve on computer. We may not be as familiar with Archimedes' trek from Sicily to Southern Italy to locate and study the legendary labyrinth which he considered to be a key-calculus unlocking the patterns of the universe.

Archimedes was aware that King Minos of Crete had come to his native Sicily centuries earlier to locate the famed artisan Daedalus and enlist him in the construction of the later-famous labyrinth of Knossos, which the King would use to imprison the Minotaur. Theseus, with the help of Ariadne's golden thread, entered the labyrinth, found his way to the prison, and slew the Minotaur.

It is my contention that this story is merely a mathematical parable to explain that man's search for knowledge reduces the bestial unknown. The labyrinth is a signal that communicates the sum of mathematical knowledge through space and time, to inform the future of the current level of characteristically human thinking, and to provide a foundation upon which the future might add its enhancements to that thinking.

As she read, the feeling came over her that she felt only when she'd discovered one of those books she *knew* must certainly be published but that her committee would turn down. She looked up at him. "Did Archimedes find what he was looking for?"

"I don't think so," Ichiro said. There was a sad note in his voice. "If he did, he left no record of it. But I believe there's still hope."

"What do you mean?"

"The cave where it was hidden was filled by debris in his time. There was no way in. But in the 1950s, the entrance to the lost cave was discovered by the Italian archaeologist Amedeo Maiuri under a vineyard. He began removing the debris. Even today the work is still in progress, but the cave is now passable, though not open to the public. I believe Maiuri saw the labyrinth and simply didn't understand its significance."

"What does the labyrinth have to do with mathematics?" she asked.

"I will show you." He reached for his pen, and drew a shape on the paper tablecloth:

"That is stage 1," he said. "We call it the generating line."

She waited for him to continue. He drew:

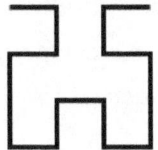

"That's the second iteration, Stage 2. Each stage of the Hilbert curve is a construction of three rotations, as Ben Trube describes: 'You simply make a mirror image of our initial stage to the right of our first stage; then make a copy of our left object and rotate it counter-clockwise 90 degrees; finally, make a copy of our right object and rotate it clockwise 90 degrees.'

"And here is the third iteration, Stage 3. As you can see Stage 3 contains 4 copies of Stage 2:"

Lisa's eyes widened. Goosebumps rose on her arms again. Her heart skipped a beat. "I don't believe this," she said.

She reached for her purse. "I came here to find out more about my roots." She retrieved the gold pendant she'd forgotten to ask Fabio about and laid it on the table next to his drawing.

His eyes narrowed in recognition. "The Greek key pattern," he said. "Or a piece of it. Which is all you need because each piece generates the whole. We topologists simply identify it with the labyrinth of infinity." The look he gave her was downright conspiratorial, as if they were meeting in a catacomb and exchanging the sign of the fish to verify their mutual Christian identity. "Where did you get that?" he finally asked. "It's the third iteration of the Hilbert Curve."

"Well, it's complicated."

"I'm complicated," he answered. "You're complicated. The world is complicated. Tell me."

She told him the story of her neighborhood bar in Brooklyn, the mysterious old man from Pozzuoli. When she mentioned the town's name, she saw Ichiro's eyes light up in astonishment.

"Pozzuoli is next to Baia," he said. "Where Archimedes searched for the cave."

"I thought it was near Cumae," she responded. "Where the cave of the sibyl is. I read about it in a novel."

Ichiro nodded. "It's the same place—they're all within a few kilometers of each other."

She went on with her story, rounding it off with the old man's "peculiar travel direction" that she go to Naples, and then picking up the pendant and the business card the next day from Sammie. "This has all been a miraculous coincidence," she concluded.

Ichiro was taking a new look at her, as though he were seeing her for the first time. "Mathematically, there can be no true coincidences. Our…intersection occurs for a reason. We have converged on this particular point, here in this room, and we must trace our trajectory together from this precise point forward." He smiled. "I am sorry, but we are meant to be together."

Lisa laughed out loud. Magic or not, she had to dispel the charge that was growing between them. "Well, I am sorry, too, but it *is* the damndest piece of serendipity I've ever seen."

Ichiro rose from the table, snapped his collar back on, and headed back to the bandstand.

His next set was a haze to her. She wouldn't even remember what songs he sang. Her mind was racing furiously, spinning with uncertainty, calculating odds, flirting with fear. Trying to figure out her reaction to this bigger than life synchronicity.

She noticed that his excitement, as he sang, seemed to increase even more—and was communicated throughout the room.

As he finished and took a deep bow, she of course joined in the hearty applause. But as he moved back to her table she sincerely hoped he wouldn't ask her what he had just sung.

"That's why I sing when I'm in Napoli," he was saying as she came out of her fog. "It's what Neapolitans do naturally. The math I can't help fiddling with. Topological conundrums keep occurring to me and my mind runs with them. It's like"—

"—It's like my writing," Lisa interrupted. "I completely understand. I just need more time."

"So you're a writer?"

"I wasn't," she hesitated, feeling her way. "In New York I edit other people's writing. But somehow here I'm writing like crazy." Her firm tone furthered her commitment. "I'm trying to let a dream come out."

Ichiro reached across the table and took her hand, held it briefly to his lips. "Brava!" he whispered. "You will continue. You must allow it. You will take your time here and write. Then I will read it. I will love it. And we will move along our line."

She recognized only decisiveness in his tone, nothing else. She didn't hurry to pull her hand back. "Your last name is Negroponte? Black bridge?" She'd never heard it.

Ichiro again became animated. "It's Greco-Italiano," he declared. "The Negroponti were among the first Greeks to settle this area. They came from Euboea."

"My name is Lisa Greco, and I'm supposedly Greek-Italian myself." She had no idea where Euboea was but for sure would look it up.

"Greco," he repeated. "I know well. Your family, like mine, were among the founding Parthenopeans." He explained that Parthenope was the ancient Euboean name of the siren who, in her despair that Ulysses wasn't attracted by her song, threw herself into the sea. "Her body washed up on the shore of what is now Naples. She was buried here. That's why even today Neapolitans call themselves after her. I can show you what's left of her ancient statue in the Archaeological Museum." His last words were hushed, dripping with future complicity.

Ichiro Negroponte seemed to know everything about his adopted city, the birthplace of his father. It reawakened in her a powerful longing to know more about this magical place of her own ancestry. Maybe the old man at Sammie's was right. "I would like that very much," she said. Even not counting the grand coincidence, Ichiro was on a quest in synch with hers—only he was many trips ahead of her. But she'd always been a quick study. She would catch up. "I did want to see Cumae," she said. "Wasn't that one of the Greeks' first outposts, too?"

Ichiro nodded. "How do you know Cumae?"

"It's described in a novel I fought to get published," she said. "It was called *The Messiah Matrix,* and it's about a man and a woman searching for scientific proof for the historical veracity of Jesus."

"How did that bring them to southern Italy?"

"They smelled the pizza from Rome?"

He laughed, without losing the intent look on his face.

81

"No, seriously," she said. "Jesus was born in the time of the Roman Empire, and the Romans believed that the cave of the sibyl in Cumae was a portal to the underworld. The story of Jesus was promulgated by the Emperor Augustus…" She stopped. "It's complicated."

"We both love complicated, remember?"

Before she could continue, the guitarist was tuning up. Ichiro rose from his chair, and reached to put on his collar. "Time for my next act." He winked at her and headed toward the waiting guitarist, who was cueing up the first notes of the next song.

Leaving Lisa to contemplate whether her claustrophobia could handle caves.

The evening ended after two, when the last guest had departed, as well as Donna Isolata and the guitarist. The tables had been cleared and Ichiro stood up again and sang *O Sole mio*, alone and only for her—a cappella as he had on the sidewalk of Quartieri Spagnoli.

Lisa was in tears as she thanked him.

He bowed, formal Japanese style, but with a flare that could only be Neapolitan. His face was bathed in perspiration.

"You must be exhausted," she said.

"I could sing all night," he said. "Especially with such an appreciative—and attractive—audience."

She stood up quickly, to distract him from her reddening face. "Thank you so much for an unforgettable evening. It's like you brought to focus all my growing feelings about Naples."

"Where are you staying?" he asked.

"I was lucky enough to find an Airbnb in a building where Rossini lived," she said.

He bowed his head. "I will walk you home," he said.

That did sound quaint and courtly to her, but she was reaching the limits of her energy and needed this night to end so she could tumble into her comfortable bed, with the French doors open. "It's a long walk," she said. "Thank you, but I'll grab a taxi."

Ichiro didn't object. He had to be at the end of his energy, too. But he insisted on at least walking her to the taxi.

When they found a cab at the corner of Via Monteoliveto, he leaned in to the driver: "Palazzo Domenico Barbaja," he directed. "*Vicino* Teatro di San Carlo." Then he turned back to her. "Rossini didn't just live there. The Teatro del Fondo virtually locked him up there until he could finish their music for Salsa's *Otello.* Your composer had been having too much fun singing and drinking with the street musicians all over town. The façade of the original Renaissance palace was crumbling, so it had just been remodeled in what Rossini considered an overly sober neoclassical style that made him refer to the place as 'my beloved prison.'" Ichiro opened the back door, and held it for her.

"You're a stellar tour guide," she said.

"Si, *cicerone superba, sono io.*" ("Yes, I am a superb tour guide").

"Ichiro, I loved this evening. Just give me some time."

"No one can give time. *You* must take your time. It's the only way."

He smiled, then turned serious. "Finish your book." Ichiro bowed, then closed her door.

She rolled her window down. "I'll imprison myself until my work is finished." Her hand was resting on the sill.

He bowed again and covered her hand with his. "I am very pleased to meet you, Lisa Greco, *Veramente piacere di conoscerti*. I was serious about my invitation."

As they drove away, she turned to watch him. With all the energy the performance must have drawn from him, she could feel the power in his dark eyes still following her.

Climbing the curved stone stairs to the door to her terrace Lisa tried to make out the face of her watch in the dim light, turning it toward her on its fraying band. "I can't believe it," she said out loud, "It's three-thirty in the morning."

She hadn't been out this late since—well, since *never*.

She opened the doors to her balcony. The full moon was emerging from behind a cloud. The music of *Marechiare* ran through her mind again. She'd figured out the first lines: *When the moon rises on Marechiaro,/ even the fish are making love*."

Sixteen

LIGHT-HEARTED AND UNBURDENED, LISA felt wrapped in joy as she stood in her long t-shirt on her little balcony and greeted the midday sun. This was the first time in her life she could remember sleeping past seven. It was strange to see the bright blue day already well underway without her. She raided the little under-the-counter refrigerator and threw together a plate of *mozzarella bagnata*, fresh tomatoes, giant almonds, basil, black olives—and the other half of the over-ripe persimmon that tasted like ice cream.

She seated herself back on the balcony that embraced the street's melodic folk songs, sweetly fragrant bakeries, and unhurried seagulls sailing coolly by at eye-level. The wood-slat table was just wide enough for her laptop, her plate, and a large cup of espresso. Taking a moment to stare down at the avenue, she could see why the novelist Stendhal had called Via Toledo "the happiest and most cheerful street in the world." But she remembered her self-imposed imprisonment, and turned with determination to her computer.

Her fingers flew freely across the keyboard pouring out the events and feelings of the last few days but shaping them to the developing story. Everything seemed to fit perfectly into the emerging pattern of what she was writing. Her fingers slowed.

What was this fear that rose from last night's encounter? A line from a D. H. Lawrence poem flashed into her mind:

The pain of loving you

Is almost more than I can bear.

Would she ever see Ichiro Negroponte again?

Maybe best to arrest the pain. "It is easier to resist at the beginning," Leonardo da Vinci said, "than at the end."

But what if she'd simply never encountered perfect?

Somehow she felt she would be seeing this unique man. Pursuing their trajectory. After all, she knew where he sang, he knew where she was staying. And maybe serendipity would call on them again. But the real question was whether she could stand it. She'd always believed that when something seemed too perfect, something was very wrong.

She forced herself to put dark thoughts aside.

For now she would discipline herself like Rossini, at least until she figured out if her book was real or just a pipe dream, a fantasy she'd clung to through the cold New York winters—that could very well dissolve on its own in the warm embrace of Naples.

It was well past two by the time she left the flat to join the people filling the avenue with constant human busyness. She'd turn right and then right again, and grab the first church that put itself in her path.

Sure enough, she rounded the corner onto Via Brigida and had walked only a few steps before discovering the carved wooden doors to the Chiesa di Santa Brigida.

Inside, she spent a few minutes admiring the Baroque paintings by Luca Giordano, whose tomb was surrounded by his uniquely-colored masterpieces: *The Glory of Santa Brigida*, *The Last Judgment,* and *The Passion*. The artwork in these churches, she surmised, must have incalculable value. But, as her author Warren Buffett would say, they possessed very little liquidity. The art, much of it frescoes, was rooted in its place for all time. You'd have to take the walls with you to steal it. No wonder the churches she'd entered so far were so well-tended. They were living museums that must cost the Holy See a fortune to maintain.

Only when she sat for meditation did she turn her eyes upward. Giordano had disguised the space's enormity by creating an artificial vanishing point, which made the dome look more human-sized, like a cupola. The clever eye lines tricked the observer's mind. She thought of Ichiro's "labyrinth of infinity" and felt the magic. She took several deep breaths to relax, pulled out her new rosary so she could run the wooden beads through her fingers, and relinquished the outside world for the quiet and peace within.

Normally her meditation was marred by hundreds of pesky thoughts—her daily to-do list, unsolved dilemmas, editorial frustrations, social issues that nagged her, adolescent memories she'd thought repressed. Today she dove easily through the stormy surface and bathed in a deep-down light as joyful as this morning's awakening. Her meditation was again one of the deepest she'd ever experienced, adding to a profound feeling of rightness.

Seventeen

SHE AIMED TO WRITE FIFTEEN pages a day before she even thought about doing anything else. In ten days she'd have cracked the back of this novel.

She'd cross the next bridge when and if she got to it.

If Ichiro was still interested then, maybe she *would* go with him to the caves. In her short time here, a fling wasn't even on the bottom of her to-do list.

She started each day with meditation on the rooftop terrace, when the morning sounds of Parthenope awakening—the chirp of birds, the barking of dogs, the garbage tenders rattling their work, the opening of shutters—receded to the horizon of her mind.

Then she climbed down the blue ladder to lose herself in her work, so lost sometimes that she didn't look up until after four p.m. Where had the time gone? From her long experience with writers and writing, she'd heard them link their art with "immortality" all too often. But, after the last few days, Lisa now clearly understood what they meant. They didn't believe they were going to live forever; they were smarter than that. Their feeling of "lostness" wasn't really immortality—how could it be? It was *timelessness,* a quality Catholics attributed only to God himself. When you were lost in your writing you felt nothing of the world's clock, and existed in a cosmos of your own creation. You were immortal in the moment. Her childbearing must not be distracted.

By the time Lisa reached her goal each day she was more than ready for afternoon meditation and a brisk walk! She'd throw together a small antipasto, gulp it down, and then pull on her shabby jeans. She'd leave the flat with no particular destination in mind. When the day came that she would normally get her hair cropped to keep it at the short length she preferred, she decided she'd skip it this time. What the hell. She was feeling more and more like an artist.

She repressed thoughts of Ichiro until she left that afternoon's church and headed toward the waterfront two blocks away, past enormous Piazza del Plebiscito where Neapolitans in 1860 had voted to join a united Italy.

Was he even real? A professor of topology, who made an annual pilgrimage to Naples to pursue ancient riddles and his hobby of opera? Hobby! The man had not an ounce of practicality in his skull. He was a dreamer, drifting through life on an aria.

But she had to admit his smile was charming, and smiled to picture it. She forced her mind in another direction, allowing distraction from her novel *only* by the colorful sights and carnival sounds

of this most accommodating city. One day she'd explore Castel Nuovo, which Google told her was built in 1279. She laughed, wondering what the Castel *Vecchio* would look like. Another day she tracked down the Cappella Sansevero where Giuseppe Sanmartino melded Baroque creativity, dynastic pride, beauty, and mystery to create the ethereal *Cristo velato*, "Veiled Christ." The reclining Christ's features, etched beneath their marble veil, were softened into the haunting impact of excruciating pain transcended by all-powerful divinity. The reclining sculpture was surrounded by guardian statues of Decorum, Liberality, Zeal, Modesty, Piety, and Self-control. The last, its marble as if colder than the others, reminded Lisa of her Manhattan self.

Though that self, as cold and mechanical as the marble, was receding into the distance. The new Lisa born of this lazy city's ease was making herself at home in her body and heart and mind. Her hair would soon be touching her bare shoulders. She'd let it grow, let it assume its natural shape, freeing her curls to their willy-nilly destinies. She poked her head into the Desigual boutique, responding to the colorfully patched jeans in the show window. They now replaced her shabby ones. And when her frayed black leather watch band finally broke after years of nervous twisting, she'd replaced it with a bright red one that already felt just right to her. She was beginning to wonder how far she would let herself go if this infernal "promotion" weren't dangling in front of her like a golden carrot.

She became a denizen of street markets, alleyway eateries in the open air, balmy weather despite the autumnal season, succulent octopus and fish on display for you to select your own, ceramic plates of *antipasti assortiti*—white to best showcase the sheer riot of colors bursting from the *abbondanza* of Campania. From old women bearing colorful paper bags against relentless waves of *motociclesti*, to young men happily balancing trays of espresso to construction sites, Lisa observed friendliness everywhere, and experienced not a moment of worry for her personal security. One night she encountered a band of young men roaming the wide avenue, arms around one another and singing with drunken abandon. She felt perfectly safe walking toward them, safe walking by them—greeted by nothing but smiles.

She was falling head over heels in love with this city, its language, its shopkeepers and restauranteurs, its street singers, roving accordionists, the varied pastel hues of its Renaissance palazzi and medieval fortresses, its mixture of Greek, Roman, French, Spanish, and Savoian monuments. The delicious wines of Campania—*Lacrima Christi* and *Falanghina* and *Greco di Tufo*—were only two or three euros a bottle. The place embodied *gioia della vita* as much in its hospitable economy as in its unending exuberance.

In New York, everywhere you looked everyone was multi-tasking; here, everyone was doing just what they were doing, doing it fully. She would ask directions to the hardware store from the *barista* where she'd stopped for a quick coffee, and instead of pointing, the young man would remove his apron and lead her up the street, down the alley, across the largo to make sure she found it. One in ten people walked along with cell phones here. In Manhattan it was more like nine out of ten.

Thinking of Manhattan made her realize her "peculiar travel" had landed her in a fateful dilemma. She would feel guilty to leave this marvelous place; and she would feel guilty if she stayed. Then she remembered something else from David Lynch's book: "It has to start from deep within, and grow and grow and grow. Then things really change."

Eighteen

SHE WAS SCRAMBLING BACK DOWN from her morning rooftop meditation overlooking Vesuvius and the golden Castel Sant'Elmo when it dawned on her that it would be a shame to waste any of these inspiring views. This morning she'd station herself on the entrance deck, at the table overlooking the austerely stately Galleria Umberto.

She finished her daily goals, more on fire than ever that the words seemed to flow from her mind as though she were doing automatic writing. As she reached the day's last paragraph, she left off in the middle of a sentence to make tomorrow's "re-start energy" minimal.

That's when Fabio showed up again, greeted her coolly, then checked her over again as though he hadn't seen her before. She was wearing cutoff jeans, a halter top, and hair that was now becoming a veritable mane. His smile widened, and she had to admit she was warming to him despite the very real possibility that he was an insatiable lothario.

"Today's the day," Fabio announced.

"Are you talking to me?" she asked, with a smile.

"I am. My friends Rosario and Anna Rosa at Antica Capri are expecting us for lunch."

The name rang a bell. She remembered, from the first day, asking him about his favorite neighborhood restaurant.

Fabio had pointed out that his favorite wasn't a *ristorante,* but a *trattoria,* and elucidated the distinction: *Ristoranti* dispensed *la cucina nobile,* at higher prices than *trattoria,* which served *cucina normale,* and were therefore preferred by locals.

"I told them I have a new guest who hasn't met them yet," he was informing her now. "You will love them, and you'll never forget the food. I assure you there's nothing *normale* about it."

So involved had she become in the writing she hadn't even nibbled this morning. Instead of scolding him for his presumption, she asked, "When?"

"*Adesso,*" he replied. "Now."

Laughing, she stood up. "Can I at least wash my face and put my laptop away?"

"Of course," Fabio said. "Though it'd be perfectly safe right there."

"And what if it rains?"

His laugh was contagious. He simply raised his eyes to the clear sky.

Meanwhile she was closing the laptop and packing it away. She changed to the colorful skirt she'd bought at a street market the other day, and exchanged the too revealing halter top for a bright purple Yale sweatshirt she'd never worn before.

If Fabio was disappointed when she emerged gypsy-dressed from her flat he didn't show it.

They crossed Via Toledo, climbed the stone staircase across from Teatro Augusto, and turned right onto the frenetic Via Speranzella. Antica Capri was a few blocks down the street. They passed a granddaughter in her teens holding hands with her mother who was linking arms with *her* mother—three generations, physically linking to pass along the knowledge of how to enjoy each day, how to *live,* how to negotiate the *motociclette* buzzing around like mosquitoes.

The exterior of the trattoria Antica Capri was dominated by an arch of stones framing a window dressed with white lace curtains and a neon sign saying "Open Pizza." Before Fabio could even reach for it, the front door popped open. Wiping his hands on his white apron, Rosario Crescenzo, compact body as efficient as his demeanor, came out to welcome them. *"Salve,"* he greeted Fabio, who returned the salutation. Rosario declared he was holding open the last table for them. After Fabio introduced her as his "writer friend" from New York, Rosario escorted them in.

Fabio insisted she sit on the wall side of the table "for the view." Lisa squeezed between the adjoining table of ten and their table for two and settled into the straw-seated chair. She liked being called a "writer," and noticed he called her "friend," not "guest," but she shrugged it off. This was Naples, after all. Why should they *not* be friends?

The red-haired waitress, named Maria, delivered the usual wine call and after making her decision for white while Fabio decided red, Lisa looked around the tiny one-room restaurant. The wall was dominated by a mosaic vista of a happy woman greeting an unseen visitor with her back turned to the deepest blue water on which the rising full moon was reflected. Bronze pots and pans of every shape and size hung above the diners who, too preoccupied by the food, took no notice. And photo after photo of happy, no doubt important, people heartily shaking hands with Rosario and his wife Lisetta, the chef.

Red-haired Maria brought quarter-carafes of wine, a color for each, and poured the first glass for them. Lisa expected a menu next.

The noisy diners were so ecstatic about their food she was eager to join them.

"Don't worry," Fabio said. "They will bring us the best and you will not be disappointed." She felt immediately more comfortable with this man, not on edge as she had with Ichiro. She tinged pink to realize that the Japanese-Italian mathematical tenor had restored himself unbidden to her consciousness.

Her host was asking her how she liked Naples so far. She responded with a waterfall of enthusiasm that, sprinkled with Neapolitan and Italian phrases, painted a very positive picture. Fabio said he was delighted to hear her favorable report, and that she must promise to return soon. The thought took her aback.

Come back? She hadn't given a moment's thought to *leaving*. And that was interesting to say the very least.

On an impulse, she pulled the pendant from her purse and showed it to Fabio.

His glance was perfunctory, his response dismissive: "*Bello*. It's very nice."

She tucked it back in her purse without a word.

"You should put it on a chain." Then he asked her if she'd been into Galleria Umberto, and seemed happy when she shook her head. "Then we will go this evening," he said. "It's one of our annual masked balls."

"Masked ball? What's the occasion?"

The hearty laugh came again. "This is Napoli," he said. "We don't need an occasion for music and dancing."

She bit her lip trying to imagine a masked ball in New York with no occasion for it except sheer celebration of life. She felt a distinct urge to see this phenomenon, but was, despite her growing sense of adventure, feeling a little cautious. She noticed again how handsome Fabio was, definitely the classic image of the Latin lover desired by every red-blooded woman who came here. Or every woman who rented one of his flats? "I'm afraid I didn't bring my mask with me," she finally said.

Fabio took it in stride. "Don't worry. I've found the perfect one for you," adding smoothly, "I will come for you at nine."

She wondered whether nine meant nine, American-style, or ten-thirty, Italian. And she wondered at his hubris, planning a date before even asking her.

As though to close the deal, Lisa's cell phone rang urgently. She swore at herself for not leaving it in the flat. Mumbling an apology to the easy-going guests and Fabio, when she saw it was from Kevin she took the call against her better judgment

"Larry Thompson's new book hit the *Times* list—and he signed with us," he gushed.

"That's great," she answered, "and *buon giorno* to you too. What time is it there anyway?"

"It's zero-dark-thirty," he answered. "You know I'm an early bird."

"And a night owl, too," she said. "I'll never understand it." His news made her remember the life she had waiting for her back in icy Manhattan. "I know he'll be pleased with Standard," she said half-heartedly.

"You don't understand. He insists that you alone be his editor, no matter what. In fact, it's a written condition of his signing. After what you did for this book on spec, he won't have it any other way."

Lisa did respect Thompson's work. Now that he'd made enough from his novels to withdraw from his law practice he had nothing to keep him from pouring his prodigious energy into one social thriller after another. His readers couldn't wait for his next one, to see what issue he'd choose after previous novels dealing with abortion rights, the greed of out-of-control pharmaceutical companies, dark campaign money, and the convolutions of the insanity plea. But she still had mixed feelings about Kevin's news. "When did you first know this?" she demanded.

"Well, a few days before you left I had lunch with Thompson's agent and she gave me a hush-hush heads up about the signing. And Phyllis just told me about making the list."

Immediately Lisa was suspicious. "Is that why the company paid for my trip?"

"I'm sure that was Phyllis' way of acknowledging good work." He tried to keep his voice level, but Lisa could hear the excitement just below the surface. "I hope you realize this puts you in the cat-bird seat."

Why was she finding it harder and harder to relate? What if where she was *at this moment* was the catbird seat? An idea began to form in her mind. "Kevin, dear man, I'm sorry to tell you this but I'm being extremely rude to my lunch companion. Congratulate Ms. Graham for me."

Kevin, of course, never failed to have the last word. "She won't be *Ms. Graham* to you for much longer," he said. "Right about now, she's worshiping your tight little ass." And hung up.

Lisa winced. Kevin knew how to annoy her. His references to her being "tightly wrapped" and having a "tight little ass" were his subtle, jocular, chauvinistic ways of recognizing all he approved about his favorite prodigy. From this transatlantic distance it just felt weird.

"Something important?" Fabio asked.

Before she had to respond, Maria arrived with their meal—and its appearance boggled the mind. It was a large dark ceramic pot that looked like an enormous chicken

pot pie but smelled more like something you could find only on Olympus. "*Pasta fagioli alla pescatora,*" the waitress announced. Before Lisa had a chance to admire the crust with its blackened bubbles, the waitress had pulled a sharp kitchen knife from her apron and sliced the baked covering off the pot, cutting it deftly into two equal parts, one for each of them. The aroma of the baked crust was pure rapture, and the smells it released from beneath it even more so; and for some reason she thought again of Ichiro. But the waitress was spooning the ingredients from the terra cotta pot onto her plate: flat  pasta strips, aromatic *fagioli* (beans), *gamberetti* (tiny shrimp), the baby fish she'd seen in the stalls marked *alici, vongolette* (tiny clams), *cozzeeca* (mussels), *purpetielli* (tiny octopus)—truly the *abbondanza* of the sea. She didn't know what to taste first. Fabio demonstrated the Neapolitan way by using his piece of crust as a shovel and scooping up the delicacies lightly bathed in tomato sauce. She followed suit.

She'd noticed glances of approval from the other diners when the waitress presented their dish.

Fabio was eating with the same smooth urbanity he seemed to bring to everything and though she wasn't sure she could feel a spark for him she certainly felt his charisma and shared his joy. Catching her eye, he wiped his lips, lifted his glass, and toasted her. What he said with his lips was "*Buon appetito,*" but his eyes said otherwise. Lisa, though mindful of her odd encounters with the effervescent Ichiro, was determined to focus on the present camaraderie. She didn't come here to fall in love, but she made no rules against a casual hookup. She came here to find herself. To experience things she'd never experienced. "*Buon appetito,*" she said back, her eyes saying he could make of this what he liked.

When they had passed the point of satiation and accepted Rosario's offer of espresso but *not* dessert, the merriment in Fabio's eyes turned naughty and he made his inelegant proposal: "Shall we go back to your flat and take a little nap together?"

"Do I excite you so much you want to *sleep* with me?"

Before he could answer, Maria appeared with the check. He reached for it. "You are my guest," he said brusquely. "But you'll have to excuse me, I'm afraid. It's time for my swim." Then he stood up and gave her the bleak smile of someone who wasn't quite sure what to do next. "*Fino alle none,*" he added. He moved the table so she could squeeze her way out. "Until nine."

At first she didn't understand.

"The ball," he reminded her.

"*Io capisc',*" she replied. "Got it." She was relieved that he was off. She didn't quite understand either. Did he make a pass, or what? Was she interested, or not? As she watched his muscular neck move toward the door, one thing was sure: if they ended up in bed it wouldn't be to sleep. What she was feeling maybe not have been magic, but it was definitely lust.

She spent the afternoon prowling the Quartieri, ruminating more over Kevin's call than Fabio's ineptness. The call made her feel like an astronaut who'd just acclimated herself to breathing the exhilarating atmosphere of an exotic new world and was now being asked to return to Earth's diminishing atmosphere. She took deep breaths, as though to clear her lungs again. Larry's signing meant she'd become more indispensable than ever. Her place at Standard was secure. Why wasn't that making her feel terrific? Instead, she could feel the dark clouds of depression gathering on her horizon. She knew she had a little time before they descended on her.

She walked by a nail salon. The young attendant was reading a picture magazine and, on a whim, Lisa asked her if she was free to do her nails. "Of course," the attendant said, indicating a large rack of colorful bottles for her to choose from. It took her only a second to select a red that nearly matched her new watchband. Maybe she'd even find red lipstick somewhere.

As the manicurist tended her hands, chattering away as though Lisa understood every word, Lisa tried to figure out what she could possibly wear to a ball she knew nothing about. As though she'd spoken the inquiry out loud, the manicurist told her they were selling costumes for tonight in Piazza Carità. Maybe she'd stroll down Via Toledo and check it out just in case inspiration might strike. When she asked her why the only people on the streets who were *not* smiling were all young men prowling at corners, the girl told her, "*Non ti preoccupar*'" ("Don't worry about it") they were *camorristi* keeping the neighborhood safe.

When she made it back to the flat, she couldn't resist opening her laptop to check her email. There were no emails from Kevin, but there *was* a brief one from Ms. Graham, reminding her that her return was now a little over a week away and hoped she was getting some rest since "your work is cut out for you when you get back. Everyone is very excited." Clearly the literary carousel she'd left behind at Standard was still spinning madly as ever. Clearly it would never stop. But Lisa wasn't ready to jump back on. She dashed a reply to Phyllis. "All's well. But actually I was about to tell you I may need a little more time here." She pushed "Send," and then closed the laptop to focus on the sunset.

Nineteen

IT WAS PROMPTLY NINE O'CLOCK when her cell phone rang again. Was it Fabio, waiting downstairs for her? Or, more likely, telling her he was running late? She picked it up to find it was Kevin instead.

He wasn't happy. "Thanks for ruining my lunch," he began. It was after lunch in New York, and Kevin would be walking back from dining with one of the literary *machers* of New York. Every day, like clockwork, day after day after day.

"What do you mean?"

"Phyllis invaded my office to tell me about the email you sent her."

Normally dread would fall upon her at this point, but Lisa felt an unusual draft of calm instead. "Yes?"

"You should *not* have written her that way," Kevin said. "You should have gone through me."

"And...?"

"She said, 'Tell her to take two more weeks. But I have to fill the position in the meantime.'"

"Well, what can I say?" Lisa didn't know how she felt about this. It wasn't relief exactly, and it wasn't elation. It was something new that she couldn't quite put her finger on.

"You can say, 'Sorry, Kevin. I didn't mean to bite a gift horse in the nose!' Do you know what you've turned down?"

"I didn't turn down anything," she said. "I just asked for a little more time. I'm working on something that might be worthwhile. I've never been more excited in my life."

"What is it?" Kevin demanded.

"If I told you about it, I'd have to kill you." She pinched herself for the feeble joke. "Seriously, I don't want to dissipate the energy I've poured into it by putting it out there prematurely. But I promise you'll be the first to know."

"I hope to hell that fat and lazy city isn't going to your head," he said, making sure his last words were emphatic before he hung up.

She'd spoken without thinking it over, but felt good about it. *This time I will take my time. I will not be jerked back into the traces before I'm ready.*

As though to underline her decision, Fabio knocked on her door. Forgetting what she was wearing, she opened it to find him dressed in a harlequin costume like the seated dummy that had frightened her back to her table at A'Canzuncella that night.

"Sorry," she gasped, realizing how he must be reacting to the surprise on her face. But his look was equally surprised.

She laughed. "What do you think?" she asked, spinning to display her costume more fully, including the red tail that she twirled in her hand. The costume fit her like a glove. She'd found the "little devil" outfit in the bustling Piazza Carità after doing her afternoon meditation in the church of Santa Maria della Carità. The Gregorian chant had brought her back to the long ago days when her Babbino had walked her to church by the hand so he wouldn't have to attend evening Benediction alone. His presence had given her the few hours of meaningfulness she'd experienced in a Catholic church— the smoke of the incense mingling with his after shave, the chant droning lofty comfort above the mumbled prayers of the congregation. So it was a throwback to her perverse rebelliousness that serendipity led her to the costume stand where the red devil's mask seemed to beckon to her. She would never, in New York, have even imagined such a thing. But here, in this city where she was freeing all parts of herself that had been disciplined into repression, it felt natural. She'd even found bright red lipstick at the adjoining stall.

"I like it," Fabio was saying. "It suits you." Dangling from his hand was the mask he'd brought for her.

The glint in his eye she chose to ignore. She stared at the dangling mask and laughed. It was a devil's mask too.

What an odd couple we must make, she thought as they entered the massive portal that led from the sidewalk of Via Toledo into Galleria Umberto—a dashing harlequin and a skinny little devil with no idea what she was doing here. She'd always wanted to wear something outrageous at some outrageous party, but never dared.

The place was bursting with humanity—and with a panoply of textures, colors, sounds, aromas. Tables formed alluring islands around the swirling partiers and offered every taste imaginable—from the sweetest of Neapolitan pastries—*Zeppole di San Giuseppe, Sfogliatelle Ricce, Sfogliatelle Frolle*

 straight from the oven, *Torta Caprese al Limone*—to the tartest of pepper-dashed *pizzette,* and *olive* of every shade of green and black. It was an overwhelming assault on the senses, though assault was hardly the right word for the sense of pure joy that pervaded the spacious gallery.

The lofty, multi-arched ceiling was like that of a cathedral, but not at all spiritual. It was a monument to worldliness, proclaiming the sheer animality of the humans who filled it tonight with vibrant laughter, shouts of recognition and salesmanship, cries of culinary joy and discovery—and, always through it and floating above it all, music.

Fabio took her hand and pulled her into the dancers, and she let herself move with him, closing her eyes as he spun her, imagining that it was five centuries ago and she was carousing with the Spanish *signori* of the Golden Age between the two eruptions of Vesuvius. His hand on her back, as he pulled her close, was exciting and she recognized that her libido was alive and well after long dormancy. But when she opened her eyes and saw Fabio's self-assured grin, she recognized something else. The sexual energy he awakened in her was not for him.

She broke their rhythm and pulled him toward the music that was drawing her like a moth to flame on the far side of the vast galleria. Slowly they made their way across the crowded space, twisting and turning through revelers and attendant vendors of cotton candy, hard candies, mementoes, and libations. Suddenly the timbre of a resonant voice became her beacon. She stopped in her tracks to be sure. Then she sharpened her pace, pulling hapless Fabio along like a puppet dragged across a stage.

The sonorous notes that had drawn her from across the gallery were coming from none other than Ichiro Negroponte. Dressed in violet priestly cassock and clown collar, his mouth was open with the rounded notes of a folk song she didn't know. He was accompanied by two men, one on guitar, one accordion.

Spotting her with Fabio, Ichiro's eyes widened as he took in her costume. She could see his brow wrinkling as his brain questioned his initial identification of the devil who approached.

His song came to an abrupt end. He bowed formerly, gave Lisa a look that was part questioning, part disappointment. Then, after a pause that filled her with fear, he broke decisively into another song.

When she recognized the new song, she realized she still had Fabio by the hand and let go. The song was "Marechiare"—only this time with words she understood:

> *When the moon pops up in Marechiaro,*
> *All the fish stiffen with love.*

Partiers who knew English burst into laughter.

> *Waves of sea, overcome with joy,*
> *Blush in every color.*
> *When moon pops up in Marechiaro!*
>
> *In Marechiaro a window beckons;*
> *My passion taps on it.*
> *Fragrant carnations sweeten air—*
> *Sea of sighs and whispers.*
> *In Marechiaro your window beckons!*
> *ah, ah, ah, ah, ah, ah, ah, ah*

The twinkle in Ichiro's eyes was unmistakable. She caught her breath; the goosebumps reappeared. The magic. She smiled back at him, bowed her head slightly.

> *Who claims stars shine bright,*
> *Hasn't seen the eyes that light your face.*
> *I alone by those bright stars*

Am blinded in my heart.

She was entranced. Had he translated the words for her, and hoped someday, randomly, to sing them to her? As though he were reading her mind, Ichiro finished:

Wake up, Lisa, smell the sweet air
Why did I wait this long?
To add music to my song
I've brought my guitar along—

The guitarist waved his guitar at her without missing a note.

Lisa, may the sweet air caress you.

Fabio's displeasure was obvious. His eyes were scanning the room. Was he embarrassed? Jealous?

She ignored him, her eyes intent on Ichiro. No one had ever sung like this to her.

Fabio walked away without a word, leaving her alone to face her serenader.

"I—I don't know what to say," she finally said, a swirl of emotions on her face.

"You don't have to say, remember?" Ichiro responded. He took her hands in his for a moment, then withdrew them.

She looked down at her hand, feeling the weight of what he'd left in it. It was a gold chain.

"For your pendant," he said. "It needs a strong chain because it is significant, for both of us."

She could see he was searching for words.

"And really quite interesting mathematically," he continued. "Because if the process of creating pattern has 'some kind of symmetry' with which it can be repeated," he faltered. "And produces finer and more complicated ones, then as a limit, we have an extremely complicated curve which can fill a rectangle or even a cube." He stumbled to an awkward silence.

"You don't have to say anything either," she said. She didn't need to understand the math but she understood the gesture. *"Ari-gato,"* she said, and kissed him on the cheek.

"I'm sorry my English isn't better. I will show you what I mean, if you permit me. I will take you there."

"I permit."

"I will come for you noon tomorrow—after your work is done." He smiled.

"To liberate me from my prison?" She looked at him.

But he didn't respond. He was staring at Fabio, who was now standing before a voluptuous blonde, antically doffing his harlequin hat at her. Ichiro's joyful expression turned to uncertainty. "You may be facing a logical crux—decisive dilemma of trajectory." He turned his gaze back to her.

"Trust me," she said. "There's no crux here at all."

Twenty

SHE AWAKENED EARLIER THAN USUAL and was already on the balcony, sipping espresso and opening her laptop to get started. Then she burst into laughter. She'd dreamed last night that she and Ichiro were seated on the ledge of the building on Via Armando Diaz where she'd seen all the lovers making out. She was in her devil costume that was now hanging on the spare bed in her room like a pirate flag; he was still dressed as a priest. "Bless me, father," she was saying, "I've been a little devil." Ichiro looked at her seriously. "And you expect me to absolve you without punishment?" he asked sternly.

She touched the geometrical pendant, now hanging on the chain around her neck, and smiled. Last night was easily the craziest thing she'd ever experienced. She remembered turning as the next song began, waving breezily to Fabio arm in arm with his new Valkyrie—his look suddenly professional and dismissive—and watching from the gallery.

She finished today's allotment well before her usual time. Checked her email. Only one, from Larry Thompson. But it was interesting:

"They don't seem to get it," the novelist wrote. "I *need* you, I *want* you, as my sole editor. Or the deal is off."

That was it? What in the world was going on at Standard? "I'm afraid I need more context," she emailed back, adding a little ☺ to show she was being friendly. Email had a way of being read with "tone," a response that always baffled her.

The return was almost immediate: "I heard that Phyllis Graham plans to let you go."

Well, that was certainly news. Where was Kevin in all this? Why hadn't he called? She checked her phone messages, and saw that he, in fact, had called. Three times.

"Phyllis is on the warpath," the first voicemail began. "She can't believe you haven't accepted the new position. She's blowing her top. Firing you. But don't worry, I'm working on it. Just hang on and I'll get back to you."

Hold on? It occurred to her in a flash that she wasn't holding on anymore. She was living a life she not only enjoyed but delighted in. If something had happened in New York that took her out of whatever limbo Phyllis thought she was in, so be it. She felt liberated, set free from a golden cage not of her own conscious choosing. The elation rushed through her like a sea change.

Like the horny moon of Marechiaro.

A new email arrived from night owl Larry Thompson. "I'm being selfish trying to keep you chained to a desk," he wrote. "Do what is right for you, Lisa, not for me, not for Standard. Tell her to shove the job. We don't need her. And send me what you've written right now. I promise I'll be constructive about it." Was that being patronizing, she wondered, or just sincere? Without hearing his voice it was hard to determine. That tone thing again.

But without letting herself overthink it, she punched the keys that launched her work through cyberspace into Larry's computer.

"This is just between us. Here's what's keeping me in Naples. I need to finish it. Am I crazy? If so, no ham no fowl." Larry loved her stupid puns. "Please be honest."

What the hell, she thought. You only live once.

Then she listened to Kevin's second and third voicemails as though they were being shouted from such a distance she could barely hear them. Something about he'd maintain his position a little longer until all was resolved and would keep her posted. Whatever.

She started an email to him, but changed her mind. Let's let my destiny make this decision, she said to herself. I'll stay out of it.

Moving like a zombie, she folded the laptop and slipped it under the mattress of the bottom bunk bed. Then she turned off her cell, and did the same with it. She would force herself to be free today. The good work she'd accomplished deserved it.

Things will work out as they are meant to work out.

She was in a happy place, another clear day had dawned, and carpe diem, seize the day, was her new mantra. Fuck them if they can't take a joke, as her Brooklyn Italian neighbors would say.

When Ichiro knocked on her door, she wasn't surprised. Everything about this man and their trajectory so far was magic.

But she must have looked surprised anyway.

"Sorry," he said, with a slight bow. "I knew the building and you described the views so I deduced you had to be on top floor."

She laughed. "Of course you did!" she said.

His driving was fast, fearless, precise. He did his best to point out
Ponti Rossi, Capodimonte, Montagna Spaccata.

But she wasn't the most attentive tour passenger, alternately curious—and terrified. "I could never drive here," she admitted. Of
course she didn't drive in New York either.

Ichiro just laughed. He was from Tokyo after all, a city that
dwarfed New York, and perfectly comfortable behind the wheel of
the rented Acura. She was, by comparison, a small-town girl. He
told her he liked her longer hair. "You look like Artemis," he said.
"Goddess of the hunt."

"I look like the devil," she responded.

"Yes, that was strangely enticing," he said, "for the eyes of a
Catholic priest." He looked at her.

She blurted it out: "I'm losing my job."

"A job is a construct," he said, taking it in stride. "A job is not
an equation, not a life. You are alive."

Now he was, what, an oracle? Not even a single question to es-
tablish context?

But on the cosmic scale at which his mind operated, Ichiro was
right. It wasn't *her* job, or *her* promotion. It was Standard's. Everything was Standard's. The corner office. The checks she was paid
with. The phones she spoke on. The computer she worked on.

"So what do I do now, Mr. Genius?" she asked.

"What you are doing," he said. "Simply what you are already
doing. Follow your passion. Write what only you can write. Proceed
where instinct or inclination lead you."

"You're one to talk," she said. "But how is that practical? How will I survive?" She studied his impassive face. "How do you support yourself? You told me your professorship barely pays your room and board in Tokyo. I'm sure your singing doesn't make you rich."

"But it will someday. When I make it to San Carlo."

San Carlo was the grand opera house of Naples, aspiration of professional tenors throughout the world. It preceded Milan's La Scala and Venice's La Fenice by decades. Lisa gave him her most serious look.

"I *am* rich already," he added. "If doing what you love is your measurement as it is mine. Seriously. Dream provides when you decide to embrace it."

"Pennies from heaven?" she asked him.

He nodded. "Exactly. Let me give you an example." He was studying her again, as if trying to decide.

"What?" she said, pressing.

"As I said, I don't believe in coincidence," he began. "But let me tell you a personal story. Do you mind?"

"By all means," she said.

"While still an undergraduate student," he told her, "I'd been obsessed with a non-Euclidean maze-game called 'Archimedes labyrinth.' After playing the game incessantly for a year I became convinced Archimedes had been on the verge of a major breakthrough involving the labyrinth. The day I decided I would spend every moment I could in Naples learning the city and my chosen art, I said to myself, 'You don't even have enough for an airline ticket. But that won't stop you. When you close the door to Tokyo, the door to Naples will open.' That was what I call 'a crossroads of commitment.' I wrote a grant proposal to the university—it later became the article I showed you—that got me to Naples for the summer. I wanted to visit the Oracle of the Dead as they now call it and see if I could locate what the ancient mathematician was seeking there. Did you know he invented integral calculus? That he irrigated his fields by making water flow uphill? And set fire to Roman warships by focusing the sun's rays through parabolic mirrors?"

Her bewildered look was answer enough, so he continued. "Of course it would be rude not to look up Donna Isolata while I was here," he grinned.

"Of course it would," she grinned back.

He could see he'd lost her and shrugged his shoulders. That was one of the crosses he cheerfully bore through life—finding no one with a clue to what he was talking about. "I guess it is a bit complicated. Better if I take you to the cave, so you can see with your own eyes what Archimedes never found. And, by the way, the student grant was later replaced with a Mellon Grant that allows me to continue my research here every year."

She stared at him in amazement. "All that from a moment of commitment?" So he wasn't such a "mad genius" after all. There was method to his madness. She would ruminate on that, learn from it, and figure out how to apply it to her own life. Because she was already feeling pretty damned good, better than she'd ever felt before. Wildly exhilarated. *This* was her life, riding into the unknown with a brilliant man. And she realized she wanted it to continue.

Clearly writing had to be her answer. Not editing. Not going to meetings. Not talking on the telephone. But *creating something* of her own, an "intellectual property." Requiring her brain and nothing else.

Her heart was filled with happiness. She realized she was there already. The novel she was writing could be her Archimedes grant. If not this one, surely the next.

She couldn't wait to get back to her keyboard. But she knew she needed to clear her thinking, that it was high time for a breather before she continued her journey. This time around, she promised herself, I will pay more attention to where I'm going.

Ichiro read her mind again. "I have to force myself to take a break," he was saying. "Much as I hate the thought. Otherwise I'd lose my voice."

The car was a warm chrysalis around them, allowing them to lose themselves in the unique rhythm of their conversation. They could feel the uniqueness of the moment and, as the emotion grew, drove in harmonious silence the next half hour.

"Where are we going? Can you tell me yet?" She was admiring the lake they were approaching, its light mist making it look surreal against the surrounding mountains.

"Some people in my field believe that the whole idea of sacred geometry is mystical nonsense," he declared without preliminary. "I am not so sure. I believe, simply, that Pythagoras and Orpheus and Archimedes argued about the same thing. That is Lake Avernus," Ichiro pointed out as though it were a sequitur. "Guarding the entrance to the underworld, according to the ancients. Therefore sacred to Orpheus, who descended into hell around here."

"Cumae?" she asked.

He looked at her and nodded. "You said you wanted to visit. It's the most ancient town of Campania, where the Greeks—our ancestors—first founded a colony. They brought Pythagorean ideas with them."

"It's where the cave of the sibyl is," she said, remembering *The Messiah Matrix,* the novel she couldn't get by her board and that went on to become a bestseller for a small California imprint.

Ichiro admitted he didn't know much about the sibyl, and she gave him a short overview of the prophetess who first became famous by carrying nine books revealing the future to Roman King Tarquin the Proud. The king refused the price she demanded, so she burned three of the books right in front of him. A year later she returned with the remaining six, and asked her original price; when the king refused, she burned another three. When she returned with the remaining three the next year, the king's advisors insisted that he pay her the original price.

"If the future could be read," Ichiro translated the story into something a mathematician could relate to: "The human brain's problem-solving capacities would never have evolved. We wouldn't need that ingenious tool."

But she had to admit it made sense. She'd never had her fortune told, her palms read, or her aura calibrated. Why would she want to know her future? It would only screw up the free will she supposedly possessed and was at this very moment trying to exercise. "I heard about the Pythagorean legend," she teased. "Something to do with right angles and triangles."

He chuckled. "It's not just a legend," he said. "It's actually an essential theorem. Without it the Athenians couldn't have built the Parthenon. But Pythagoras was more than a geometrician and mathematician. He was convinced the universe was generated from numbers, and that each number resonated with its own individual vibratory pattern—the combination of all numbers producing what he called 'the music of the spheres.'"

The gooseflesh reappeared on her arms and she crossed them to hide it. "I read that the ancient Hindus believed that '*Om*' was the heartbeat of the universe, or something like that."

Ichiro nodded. "*Om mani padme hum.* The perfect sound, generating the universe. Pythagoras influenced the Hindus and Buddhists. They were obsessed with numbers. Some of the best mathematicians in the world are from India."

"I thought Orpheus was the god of music," she said.

"According to legend he was the first musician. His lyre was so powerful that trees wept to hear him play it, animals followed him, and even the moon and sun shone brighter."

"Reminds me of *Marechiare,*" she laughed. "Thank you again for translating that naughty song for me. That was a very thoughtful thing to do. How did you know you'd see me again?"

"I didn't *know* it precisely," he said. "But I knew you made a very strong impression on me that I would not forget. The rest," he paused, "was up to the retroactive purposefulness of apparently random patterns."

"You mean meandering is sure to lead to discovery?" It had suddenly occurred to her that her pendant was itself "a peculiar travel suggestion" that had led her, willy-nilly, indirectly, and serendipitously, to this very moment. A point in time and space.

"Besides what I knew or didn't know, I *felt* I would have found you, no matter what."

Their eyes met.

She took his hand, and held it in her lap.

"We'll have to hurry if we're going to check out your cave as well as the one I wanted you to see at Baia." He was looking at the sun on the horizon, trying to gauge the time.

"Are they far apart?" she asked.

"Not so far on the map," he said. "But these little side roads are tricky and not always in perfect repair. And it takes time to walk to the sites once you've parked the car."

"I want to see the one you wanted to show me. Don't worry about the sibyl's cave."

"No, we'll check it out first. I'd very much like to see it. Then we can spend the rest of the day in Baia at the cave archaeologists now identify with the Oracle of the Dead."

"Now *that* sounds like fun," she said.

They passed a road sign for Cumae. Lisa's heart beat faster to think she was nearing the area the dapper man at Sammie's insisted she visit, where her remote ancestors first landed when they emigrated from Greece for Italy. A few more kilometers, and they were parking in the tiny lot facing the entrance stand to the ruins, its plaque identifying it as Parco Archeologico di Cuma—Antro della Sibilla.

Lisa noted that *The Messiah Matrix* author didn't describe the modern entrance booth where maps and mementoes were being sold, and where they paid the 2€ entrance fee; nor the wire fence that flanked the 100-yard path to the cave, with diagrams of the excavations along the way.

Well, the author made the right decision.

Fiction is as much about what you leave out as it is what you put in. It was much more romantic the way he had it. The fence and diagrams risked reducing the magic of the place to practical reality.

But her feeling of letdown evaporated when, crossing beneath an ancient stone arch, the actual cave came into sight. The symmetry

of its unique recessive arches took her
breath away. This is what Virgil meant by its
"hundred mouths." She looked to Ichiro for
his reaction.

He, too, appeared to be in awe. "It is always curious to me how human construction, when it attempts sacred geometry,
imitates structures already established by nature."

"And what natural structure would you say this imitates?"

He looked at her. "Precisely," he said, "the birth canal. The entrance to the womb."

She blushed. "I didn't realize you were an expert on female anat-
omy."

He sidestepped the comment. "Geometry and mathematics are
part of humanity's search to define beauty, and our very concept of
beauty comes from nature. That is why some call it 'sacred geometry.'"

"Why didn't I hear about sacred geometry in high school?"

"According to Robert Ferré, sacred geometry is 'the act of studying the divine act of creation and then using that knowledge to
create in the same way.'" He paused to see if she wanted to hear
more, then continued: "When we observe nature, we discover that
the basic building blocks of creation are geometric. The creator's
hand is responsible for originating numbers and proportions in the
manifest universe. Studying sacred geometry leads us to truth and
self-understanding. All societies use sacred geometry to construct
their temples, sacred places, and art: the Great Pyramid of Giza, for
example, or the Parthenon in Athens, or the Pantheon in Rome, or
the Pyramids of the Sun and Moon outside Mexico City, or Da
Vinci's geometrical anatomies, or Iran's Nasir Al-Mulk Mosque, or

the Great Wall of China, or any decent Roman aqueduct. Numbers aren't just for counting, nor are they just symbolic. They're embodied in the material form of everything that exists—from the spiral of a snail's shell, to the honeycomb, to the snowflake, to the lotus root, to a cross-section of red cabbage. And what we construct can honor the aesthetics of nature by imitating—and perhaps exceeding—it."

"I could listen to you forever," Lisa said, meaning it. "Even when you're *not* singing." If her high school algebra and geometry teachers had spoken this way she'd have been fascinated by math instead of baffled and repelled.

"What is that American saying? 'Be careful what you wish for.'" He laughed.

She looked into his eyes, measuring and calibrating.

They took their time entering the cave, moving slowly from the largest arch, at the opening, toward the distant smallest and final arch.

Along the way, Lisa noted that the cave was illuminated perfectly by side-shafts carved into its exterior walls to capture sunlight and focus it on the interior passageway. The very concept of this cave *was* beautiful, a perfect enlistment of geometry and purpose. It *was* sacred geometry, making her feel empowered to think humans were capable of such applied and discipline *imitation*, even if it was in service to their gods. Maybe their gods were only representations of the ideal for which humans have strived from the beginning.

"So this is where Odysseus descended into Hades?" she asked. "And Aeneas—and Orpheus?"

"I'm not so sure. Maybe Aeneas, because Virgil's description is very close to what we see here. But it's the other cave I wanted to show you that Odysseus and Orpheus probably descended."

Ichiro took her hand as they approached the final chamber, and she responded with a squeeze and a smile. "I'm honored you allowed me to bring you here," he said. "It's a monumental example of a 'Mandelbrot set.'"

She gave him her look.

"'Fractal geometry.'" He took his cues from her facial reaction. "Fractal means the dimension of the figures are not necessarily integers, but can be fractal numbers, like 1.5, or log 4/log 3, etc., but in a way that they manifest 'self-similarity.' Heisuke Hironaka, who by the way was awarded the Fields Medal, described to me a very fundamental and simple, but really mathematical, motivation for fractal geometry for Mandelbrot."

"I'm afraid you're losing me."

"Imitating the creator of the universe, who created microscopic atomic structures that mirror enormous star systems, each figure in a Mandelbrot set must contain a smaller part which is really similar to itself, that implies it contains similar and arbitrarily smaller parts infinitely."

Lisa flashed back to her Yale classes on Dante. "You mean the whole and the parts reflect each other perfectly."

Ichiro nodded his approval. "Yes, and this geometrical symmetry transmits the mystical to us, the sacred—a sense of infinity."

She understood. It's why she felt a physical chill when she reread a line of Dante's *Commedia* until she truly comprehended it, as if it was putting her in direct touch with something transcendent—something Dante identified as "the divine."

Standing together in the center of the chamber, she looked at Ichiro and realized that in her wildest dreams she'd never imagined she could be chatting casually with a theoretical mathematician. Thank God for his singing. It made him less intimidating.

He looked back at her seriously, but the playful glint soon returned to his eyes. "Let's test the validity of the acoustic construction." He let go of her hand, opened his arms and broke into song:

When whippoorwills call, and evenin' is nigh

I hurry to my blue heaven

Just turn to the right, find a little white light

That lead you to my blue heaven!

She burst into laughter. She could feel the warmth, her spirit embracing his.

Twenty-one

THEY DIDN'T MAKE IT TO Ichiro's oracle that day. Ichiro was confessing his lifelong fascination with American pop music as they were ascending back beneath the trapezoidal walls of the womb-like cave—when a thunder and lightning storm broke out like neither of them had ever witnessed. The rush of wind and the overpowering scent of ozone hammered them with chill potency. While the receding arches—the hundred mouths Virgil wrote of—allowed sun from their flanking skylights to illuminate the pilgrims' path, they also allowed rain in.

They were fortunate to find a side chamber with a full ceiling and scurried into it. Neither had dressed to face elements as primal and relentless as this. Ichiro put his arm around her almost apologetically.

She accepted the warmth freely and huddled in its shelter, hoping her body offered equal comfort to his. As time passed, despite the protestations and demands for attention from the howling storm which clearly had no intention of stopping anytime soon, their body warmth became the only reality. The energy radiating between them was unique, one which neither had experienced and both treasured. Lisa felt an overwhelming urge to burrow as deeply into her private guide to the underworld as he would allow. But she feared breaking the spell that had not only brought them together but also was keeping them safe from the tempest. Instead, she slipped into meditation and, for the twenty minutes of her deep and regular breathing, there was silence between them while she wandered alone but not alone through the realms of light within.

Until Ichiro broke the spell. "We don't want to be trapped here all night," he said. "I will make a run for the car and bring it to where the stone steps begin. When you hear the horn beep, you can run down and meet me."

"And be rescued in your rented chariot like a princess?" she said. "Is that the idea?"

He laughed. "Sure. Why not?"

"I'm going with you," she declared. "I'm not going to stay here alone and dry while you brave the elements."

"Why?"

"I—I'm a little claustrophobic," she finally confessed. "But only when I'm alone."

Ichiro let it go. "I've noted the wind has been dipping every once in a while, before returning to full force," he said. "We'll wait for the next dip, and—"

"—Run like hell?"

He hugged her close again.

The next dip came a few minutes later. Pulling her up, Ichiro led the way down the surreal octagonal tunnel. Their clasped hands allowed them to save each other from the slips and slides that were inevitable on the rain-soaked flagstone path, but even when they reached the modern concrete roadway neither felt like letting go.

The gap in the wind didn't quite last long enough. By the time they reached the car, they were drenched through and through. The tears in her eyes were mixed with rain. This storm was just flexing its muscles, and showed no sign of abating.

Ichiro breathed a sigh of relief when the windshield wipers instantly busied themselves to clear the windows. "Thank God for Japanese engineering," he grunted.

"Yeah, if this were a Ford we'd be in trouble."

He laughed.

Her top was clinging to her, and she hoped he wasn't noticing her nipples hardened by the drench.

Although it was only 4.9 kilometers to the nearest town, it took them nearly an hour to find their way to Pozzuoli—through enormous puddles in the road, flooded intersections, and torrents from the hillsides bearing boulders to further imperil the roadway. Lisa watched his eyes as he navigated between Scylla and Charybdis like the hero Odysseus who visited the underworld here long before them. She noticed that the intensity in Ichiro's demeanor was not caused by fear, but by the thrill of the challenge. It's his mathematical genius, taking every turn in their trajectory as a calculus to be worked through, analyzed, and solved. I wonder what he would do if he had a blackboard?

He allowed himself a glance her way, a glance that rose to a question mark.

"You are handling this drive as though it were a matter of life and death," she explained.

"*Sumimasen,* I apologize. I've always taken things seriously." He shrugged his shoulders and relaxed.

But not for long. A truck barreling toward them swerved into their lane. Ichiro's reaction was lightning-fast. He swerved around the oncoming projectile and although their right wheels went off the road, he made sure they did so on firm ground. The truck roared past with a mighty whoosh that Lisa could feel physically, as the Acura, buffeted by its wash, shuddered. "Are you all right?" he asked.

"Thanks to you, I am," she said, taking his free hand in hers and giving it a squeeze. "No complaints about your driving from my direction," she said. "You saved our lives."

"It was logical reaction to necessity," he shrugged. "A trajectory bearing that weight and displaying that speed could not be on intersecting course with a lighter object at a lesser speed. I therefore simply changed our trajectory in case he did not change his."

"And what if he *had* changed his trajectory, to avoid us, in the same exact direction as you changed ours?"

"Unnecessary overthinking is counterproductive." He looked at her. "I simply assumed I was thinking faster. That's why I'm being very serious."

They stopped at a clothing store that was open despite the continuing torrent that threatened to close the road. It was a nondescript little establishment that seemed to offer anything and everything its owners ran across. They emerged each carrying a bundle and smiling, having agreed to stop at the first lodging in Pozzuoli they came across.

Lisa's memories went back to her Babbino, who long ago had reminisced about this very town *"su' mar',"* by the sea. "A tear would come to my grandfather's eye, and he would wipe it away as though to rid himself of a sentiment immigrants must put aside."

"That's it," she shouted. "Stop here." She reached into her purse and withdrew the business card the dapper man had given her through Sammie.

The Hotel la Tripergola was nearly obscured with rain and mist. It directly overlooked the harbor—when you could see it. All they could make out now were jigsaw-like pieces of mast and hull tossed by wind. But this was the place the old man in Brooklyn had wanted her to know about.

Ichiro parked the Acura as close to the entrance as he could, to shorten their dash inside. The receptionist, an ancient man with a timeless face that reminded her of Buddha, wore professorial tortoise-shell glasses that made his eyes seem like disapproving saucers. He greeted them with barely disguised skepticism touched with horror as, still drenched, they squished their way across his impeccably clean marble lobby.

"Ci dispiace" ("We're sorry"), Ichiro began. "We've been caught in the downpour and need to dry out." He lifted his clothes bag as though to explain all.

"Volet' una cammar', o duje?" ("Do you want one room, or two?") the man asked.

"Una, per favore," Lisa said promptly, sparing Ichiro the embarrassment of asking her the uncomfortable question.

Ichiro and the clerk gave her the same look, which she met with a disarming stare that moved the old clerk into action—slow action, but action nonetheless. He was reaching for an old-fashioned oversized key marked "9," and handed it to Ichiro, pushing a single piece of paper toward him at the same time. She was watching him, thinking he looked vaguely familiar.

"I'll fill it out," Lisa said, reaching for a pen in her bag.

"*Passaporti, ppiacere,*" he requested, his accent thick.

Ichiro's shrug was classic. "We drove up from Napoli for the day," he explained in his nonchalant Italian. "We didn't plan on being caught in the storm or spending the night."

Lisa handed him the business card.

The clerk studied it as though it were an ancient manuscript, then glanced back at her, as though he were evaluating homeland security risks.

"A stranger gave me the card, and told me I must look up this place if I came to Pozzuoli," she explained.

"*Va be',*" he finally said, with a shrug. "I accept credit card instead."

They repressed a laugh, as though the workaday words were being spoken by the judge of the afterlife. She let Ichiro dig into his wallet and retrieve a MasterCard with cherry blossoms on it. He handed it over. The man received the card as though he'd lost further interest in this couple he didn't need to understand. "Please be careful," was his dismissal; and it was clear he meant careful not to mess up everything. He handed over the key, a "9" dangling by a chain.

"Dragon number, 3 x 3, sacred to emperor, 'long-lasting,'" Ichiro said solemnly.

"Cloud nine," Lisa teased.

They squished their way up the terra cotta stairs to find Room 9, balcony and all, facing the front of the hotel and the port. Lisa noticed the immediate comfort between them—as though they weren't strangers about to be alone in a hotel room for the first time, but teenage pals following the rules of adventure—and practicality.

She marched into the bathroom looking for towels and re-trieved the two thin ones she found. "I'm afraid these will have to do," she said, handing one to Ichiro. "Why don't you use the bath-room first? That way I can do my afternoon meditation."

Ichiro refused, a look of consternation on his face that indicated going first was unimaginable. "I insist," he said. "I will figure out our situation and how to improve it. My cell phone has three bars so Google should be working."

She was still glad she had left hers behind, and chuckled at his earnestness. "Thank you. You do that. I won't be long." She re-treated to the tile bathroom and spotted what looked like a radiator on the wall. Sure enough, turning the black knob produced barely discernible heat—but warmth nonetheless. She parked her towel on its ridges and peeled off the clothes that were clinging to her. She wrung them out over the shower floor, and hung them on the re-tractable clothesline. In a sudden moment of modesty, she hung her thong *beneath* her blouse. Would he think she didn't *wear* panties if he couldn't see them? She laughed at herself. If he now knew she wore no bra? She felt, as always, embarrassed by the smallness of her breasts and wanted to keep them hidden from his eyes, if her nipples would just cooperate.

When it finally warmed up, the shower was the perfect antidote to the chilling rain. It bathed her in the warmth she felt inside until outer Lisa matched inner Lisa again. Her face was rosy as she emerged into the scant comfort of the towel. But the towel got the job done, and she turned to her clothes package.

She emerged from the tiny room a new woman, leaving the door open to disburse the clammy human odor. The denim-colored blue shift she'd found at the store felt infinitely better than the wet-tight jeans, its loose fit making her feel more feminine than she remem-bered feeling in ages. "Okay," she said. "I warmed it up for you."

"Arigato," he said, his eyes narrowing. He took his time appraising her, as though it were official business. "You—you look *kire-ina*...Beautiful, *bellissima,*" he exclaimed with all the solemnity of an officiating bishop.

She colored. "Go away," she said, waving him toward the bathroom.

She used the time to meditate again, sitting on the one chair that she pulled to face the sea that was now gradually emerging from heavy clouds. With no idea except excitement about what might happen next, Lisa still had a good feeling about it all. She settled into her mantra, closing her eyes and delving within. When, she opened them again at the click of the bathroom door, she realized four things simultaneously:

Ichiro, now in dry chinos and dark blue dress shirt, was quite a dashing guy.

She was perfectly comfortable with him.

She was also a little afraid.

And she was starving.

Buddha clerk was right on. He'd asked them only how hungry they were, and they'd both responded, "Very." La Fattoria del Campiglione was a dead serious country restaurant, a shrine to *"il culto delle carni"* ("the cult of meat") bearing its designation *Antica Osteria* with pride and confidence. It was a place for robust appetites, with no attempt to cater to dieters. From her first glance at the guests' heaping plates, Lisa knew vegetarians would find little tolerance here.

They were greeted by the owner, who, perched at the front desk in a green smock and jaunty cap, seemed to be conducting his domain like an orchestra. Across from him was a long wooden table displaying the evening's offerings—every cut of beef imaginable, darkly marbled and perfectly aged and unapologetic. The proprietor took one look at them and escorted the handsome young couple to the single table open by the fireplace. "*Mettetevi comodi*" ("Make yourselves comfortable"), he gestured with a flourish of his arm, holding the chair for Lisa until she seated herself.

"*Prego, signore,*" Lisa said. She loved this place already, wondering if they even served salads. As a gal from provincial Buffalo, she'd never fully adjusted to the health fads of Manhattan that were even creeping over to Brooklyn. The first thing she spotted was the big white banner in English: "Slow Food," symbolized by a snail's shell. She gave Ichiro a happy smile. His eyes confirmed they would take their time here. They were in no hurry.

They were surrounded by sweet-scented beeswax candles, the gentle light flickering on copper pots, brightly-colored cowbells, and farm tools that decorated the beige walls. Ichiro's eyes seemed glazed. "Are you lost in your clouds?" she asked.

"I'm lost in the moment," he responded at once. "I am in an eatery that my parents would consider paradise, with an angel in blue I could never have conjured up in my wildest dreams."

"Why paradise?" Lisa deflected the compliment.

He nodded at the refrigerated showcase displaying cuts of meat labeled as "Argentina," "New Zealand," "Kentucky," and "Japan"; as well as "Chianina," "Romagnola," "Podalica," "Marchigiana," and "Maremmana." "In Japan, just *one* of those steaks would serve ten people," he said. "We might as well be in Texas," he added with a hush of reverence in his voice.

"Have you been to Texas?" She had not.

"Only in my daydreams," he said. "There's a restaurant called 'Big Texan' there that serves seventy-two ounce steaks. If you can eat the whole thing, you don't have to pay. But I've heard they aren't big on topological geometry."

Lisa laughed. She felt the warmth bathing them from the fireplace and shivered to remember how cold she'd been when they'd arrived at the hotel. "I'd love some soup," she said, noticing a steaming bowl being served at the next table. Their waiter appeared and she pointed. He nodded.

Returning with two bowls, the waiter told them the soup was "Circerchia Flegrea" and called it a "*piatto povero*" ("poor plate"), a dish eaten by local *paisani* from time immemorial. It was incredibly tasty, with hints of chestnut and barley. The cold of the storm evaporated from her cellular memory as she sipped the country broth, dipping into it with the warm-from-the-oven, paper-thin pita. "This *is paradiso*," she exclaimed.

Ichiro was deep in conversation with the waiter, who was, after serving them a small platter of dark-purple Kalamata olives "grown right here behind the restaurant," informing him that the soup was Neolithic, its recipe going back to Mycenaean times and imported with them by exiles from Euboea: bay leaf, rosemary, broth from smoked pork ribs served on legumes that also dated back to antiquity—a cross between *ceci,* chickpeas, and regular peas.

"The roots of our cuisine," he was proclaiming, "were the sophistication of Greek kitchens merging with the simplicity of Roman *cucina.*"

When Ichiro assured the waiter—whose name was Giovanni—"We are entirely in your hands, *Siamo del tutto nelle tue mani,*" Giovanni recommended they try the mussels next.

A few minutes later he delivered mussels spiced with cumin, savory, and fenugreek accented with leeks, baby onions and raisins, carrots, celery, and dried orange peel. Seeking Giovanni's advice on the wine, they resolved it should be Piedirosso. The waiter nodded solemnly at the decision, and explained the choice was the ancient local favorite; its origins, too, lost in Greco-Roman history when the vines were first introduced to the harsh soil of the area, rich in ashes, lapillus, and tufo. The area was named the Phlegraean Fields by the Greek settlers because of the smoke and flames that rose from the volcanic soil.

Lisa was getting used to what appeared to be the Campagnian ritual of speaking of each meal almost ceremoniously as though it were the most important of your life.

They relished each sip of the deep red wine, decrypting its blackberries, sage, and edgy hint of ash.

It was indeed a splendid wine. Lisa felt this was truly the first time she'd really *tasted* a wine in way that registered fully with her. It could have been the place and the company, she mused. Or the unique combination. They clinked glasses.

"Here's to the surprise storm," she said.

"*Kanpai!* To the sacred geometrical synchronicity that brought us together," Ichiro added, tilting his glass toward her pendant.

"And the number nine." She dared a naughty grin.

Ichiro looked away.

Following the mussels, Giovanni brought them two perfect ravioli each, explaining they were stuffed with cream sauce which he called "Circerchia Flegrea Me'lanurka Quarto," another recipe dating back to "the ancient Roman cookbooks attributed to Apicius." She tasted something that was firm and crunchy, with a sweet aroma and a pleasantly acidic taste. Giovanni told them it was the Anurka, a special apple of the region—depicted on the frescoes of ancient Pompeii. It, too, was imported by the Greeks. *I Greci.* The Grecos.

Her family name was an everyday word here.

"I've never tasted anything like it," Ichiro said. "Except maybe cherry blossom stems."

Between each course, a single slice of the dehydrated apple, sprinkled with grated cinnamon, was served to cleanse the palate.

"I do believe in serendipity," Lisa said. "You will find it more in zig zags than in straight lines. I get my happiest moments—just walking around that way. I guess I *am* a meanderer at heart. Or at least I'd like to be."

Ichiro was staring at her. "So you must understand," he said, "the two of us form the gold thread into the labyrinth. We have wandered here together for the purpose of bringing our infinite potential to life."

She was touched. His words echoed what she'd been writing, but his in an even more precise way. That was his mathematical training. She would learn from it, incorporate some of it in her work. She fingered her pendant. "You called this the *meander* pattern," she said. "Tell me more about it."

He told her that the meander was the most important design in ancient Greece, symbolizing infinity, "the eternal flow of things. Many temples and artifacts were decorated with the motif, and it was well known that it dated back to the labyrinth of Knossos in Crete or even earlier. The ancient Greeks named it that after *Meandros,* the river in southern Turkey that snakes its way to the sea repeatedly doubling back on itself."

"Maybe it's in no hurry to lose itself in the sea," Lisa said.

Ichiro nodded as though agreeing with what he just said. "It's the pattern of intersecting and reflecting planes. Some theorists at N.A.S.A. even believe it may hold the key to space travel."

"The Greco key?" she teased.

But the seriousness on his face didn't flicker. "On the astronomical level, the straight line between distant objects, as distance approaches infinity, may not be straight. That's why we—topologists—call even angles 'curves.'"

Her intuition was telling her it made practical sense. The concept may have baffled others but it was suiting her own view of life perfectly. She'd recognized a long time ago that anywhere she'd reached that was unique or the least bit magical she'd reached by accident or indirection. Like the day she stumbled on little Paley Park on East 53rd, or the abandoned City Hall subway station she'd discovered when she forgot to get off the 6 Train.

"The god Meandros must be your guardian spirit," Ichiro said playfully. "But did you know he was also the grandfather of Parthenope?"

His eyes demanded a response. Lisa remembered the name—the siren—Parthenope, for whom ancient Greek Naples was named. Her gooseflesh returned. There was much sorting to do, she understood. And she could think of nothing more fortunate than being able to sort it together with this unique man who'd meandered by her table on her first magical evening in Naples. But the fear was creeping up again, sending a bone-deep chill through her. She looked at him, with no effort to hide the tears in her eyes. "Let's take it slow," she finally said.

"It was a very slow river," he replied, "as you said, reluctant to lose its identity in the sea."

She could think about that more later.

By the time they got to the main course, Lisa was relieved that Ichiro ordered the Kobe beef. She was still hungry, but not enough to tackle one of the roast-sized cutlets on grandiose display in the cooler.

The Kobe was suitably diminutive, enough for three thin slices each, served with a dollop of wasabi and three sliced bright orange Roma tomatoes. The meat was aged, marbled and barely charred. Perfection. "I've never eaten anything so yummy and tender in my life!" she exclaimed.

"I'm relieved," Ichiro said. "I was afraid you were waiting for a giant ribeye."

"Because I'm an American?" she asked, her eyebrow rising in challenge.

"Americans do like to eat," he said, his tone non-committal.

Instrumental music had started and now filled the room of chattering diners with hearty authority that reduced them to silence by perfectly reflecting their ecstasy. It began with *Tosca*—Ichiro identified it for her.

When the second piece started, Ichiro recognized it from the first beat and clinked her glass again, his eyes meeting hers with that intensity that needed no words.

He stood up, took his modest bow, and awaited the right bar. When he opened his mouth, the diners put their forks down with astonishment. Then they—and she—began to clap in time.

> *Libiamo, libiamo ne'lieti calici*
> *Che la bellezza infiora.*
> *El la fuggevol ora s'inebril a voluttà*
> *Libiam ne'dolci fremiti*
> *Che suscita l'amore,*
> *Poiché quell'ochio al core onnipotente va.*

135

Libiamo, amore, amor fra i calici
Più caldi baci avrà
Libiamo, amore, amor fra I calici
Più caldi baci avrà

La Traviata was one of the few operas she'd seen more than once. The first time was when her Babbino had wrangled permission from her parents and taken his only and favorite granddaughter by Amtrak to New York to spend one night at the Waldorf Astoria after attending the Metropolitan Opera on Manhattan's West Side. They left Buffalo Saturday morning on the earliest train and managed to just make the eight p.m. performance because the train was delayed, the scheduled eight hours taking eleven. Though later visits to the city would blur into the everyday frenzy of her Yale years, this earlier visit stood out in her memory like a diamond sparkling among costume jewelry. They'd taken a taxi from Grand Central and made it to Lincoln Center ten minutes before curtain, checking their one bag at the cloakroom and waltzing in as though they were normal opera-goers who'd just sauntered over from dinner.

One of the most vivid memories of her growing up was the excitement of that whole day, the seriousness of the old man's commitment to delivering this experience to her. Lisa would never forget the tears rolling down her grandfather's cheeks as he listened, rapt, to the sonorous music that resounded through the elegant hall and filled them both with exhilaration.

Only yesterday she'd been on Via Giuseppe Verdi, around the corner from Teatro San Carlo, picking up a mineral water—thrilled to walk a street named after the great composer of her favorite opera. When Lisa moved to New York from Connecticut, she'd promised herself that she'd never fail to see the opera again whenever it played nearby. She'd seen it three times, studied the libretto until she knew it by heart:

Let's drink, let's drink from joyful goblets
Since beauty is now in full bloom
And let the fleeing hours intoxicate us
As we taste the sweet thrills Love arouses,
Let our eyes follow our hearts.
Let's drink, my love, till love from our chalices
Makes warmer kisses.

It was as though Ichiro and the moment had conspired to fill her heart—with memory, with music, with this place, and with him. She felt her grandfather's tears burning in hers and did not hold back. She had brought them home.

When he finished the aria, Ichiro bowed to the diners who were rising to their feet to celebrate his appearance among them. Instrumental music from Verdi's opera continued, and the diners moved to the space among the tables and began to dance to this dramatic song of exuberant celebration. Of course she couldn't refuse his hand when Ichiro almost shyly turned back to her. He led her into the dancers, and relaxed by the fine Piedirosso, they found their place among them.

Feeling his arm on her back filled her with shivers and she pulled him closer with hers so she could whisper in his ear. "You have no idea how much this means to me, thank you. I wish I were Violetta tonight to share this cheerful time with you." She whispered Violetta's words:

Everything is crazy, crazy in this world
That's not pleasure. Let's embrace it all,
Fleeting and fast is the joy of love,
A flower that blooms and dies
And then can't be enjoyed.
Let us enjoy, while it's calling us
In its passionate accent.

Ichiro turned his head so he could look directly in her face. It was the moment.

But there was hesitation on both sides, and trepidation on her part.

And the music stopped.

The moment passed.

When the dancers resumed their seats at the tables, Giovanni appeared at theirs holding a small wooden tray. As though in response to the imagery of the aria, the tray contained two goblets holding a bright yellow liqueur. "Limoncello," he announced with a grave smile.

They reached for the festive crystal glasses eagerly, as though they were both intent on prolonging the evening—and in postponing what might come next. After they had toasted and savored the sweet citrus liqueur, without being asked, Giovanni refilled their glasses. This time they sipped slowly looking into each other's eyes without speaking, filling their senses with the warmth and joy that radiated through the room.

Neither of them, next morning, would remember the return to the hotel, or the lobby, or the staircase to Room Number 9. They were beyond exhausted. Both had purchased long camouflage matching t-shirts at the countryside clothing store, and when Ichiro returned from the bathroom wearing his, they both suppressed a giggle. He pulled a pillow from beside her, and was about to toss it on the couch, where he'd already installed the extra blanket he'd taken from the closet.

Lisa watched what he was doing: "Don't be stupid," she said, her voice a bit slurred with fatigue, alcohol, and nerves she tried to hide. "I need your warmth. Come over here. It's too cold to sleep apart."

He moved toward the bed.

She pulled back the covers on his side as he climbed in.

"And you need to kiss me now. Take your time."

Twenty-two

THE SUN STREAMING IN FROM the balcony awakened her. She rubbed her eyes, then reached from habit for her watch on the bedside table. It all came back to her and she turned to Ichiro's side. He was still asleep, breathing gently, innocence etched on his relaxed face. She had no idea how long their kiss had lasted. They must have fallen asleep in the middle of it because she could only remember the tentativeness—and tenderness—of its beginning, the nibbling that slowly mounted to passion until they were locked in profundity of their own creation. She remembered the sweetness of being lost in him, of feeling his tongue entwined with his, communicating on a level that transcended words and music. She remembered wanting it to never end—and then remembered nothing else.

But she felt rested and ready for the day, and filled with that feeling of rightness that came upon her lately only when she was writing. She pulled off her t-shirt, threw on her smock, and started to head for the door.

"*Nanji desu-ka?* What time is it?" the sleepy voice croaked.

"It's our time," she answered, touching his face. "I'll be right back."

She could smell the coffee on her way down the stairs. She followed her nose to the kitchen, where a young woman in a black apron greeted her.

Then, tray at hand, she was back at Room 9 with two cappuccinos.

Ichiro was fully awake. "*Grazie mille,*" he said as she handed him a cup.

"What do you take in your espresso?"

He shook his head. "*Niente.* Nothing."

She walked to the balcony doors, and opened them. "It's a beautiful day," she said. "No sign of the storm."

Still in his t-shirt, Ichiro made his way to the chair opposite her. For a moment they sat in silence, sipping the coffee and staring out at the colorful boats that filled the harbor, and at the island-studded sea beyond.

"Ships bearing our ancestors landed right here after their voyage from Euboea," Ichiro said.

"That's just what I was thinking."

He took her hand.

Before he could speak, she freed her hand and touched his cheek. It was no longer smooth. He had a morning beard. And it only made him handsomer.

"I have to be honest with you. I'm not sure I'm ready for this," she said.

Ichiro took that in, finished his espresso. "Ready for what? Ready for a beautiful day? Ready for breakfast? Ready for light-borne dynamic Archimedic spirals driving periodic oscillatory patterns into topological solitons of anisotropic soft matter? Ready for a voyage into the labyrinthine future? Ready to meander our way to the next step on our trajectory together?"

She laughed and raised his hand to her lips. And kissed it. "I still have a lot of sorting out to do. I need to clear my mind."

"All it takes for clear mind is for you to clear it," he said.

If only that were true. Her meditations were an endless struggle to find the clarity of light beneath all the ceaseless thoughts. But right now she was mesmerized by the power in his eyes, the decisiveness that radiated from him—and stopped him with her mouth.

His mouth, surprised, took a few moments to relax enough to respond. Then she felt his hunger. This kiss was filled with promises, made and taken back, chased and chasing, celebrated and regretted.

Finally she tore herself away. "At this particular point, I don't have time for a relationship I'm afraid," she said. "Can you try to understand that?"

"You mean you just want sex?" His voice was playful.

"Not really. Well, maybe. Kind of."

He stood and walked around the table, leaned over and put his arms around her.

She turned her head to kiss him again. This time his kiss was more urgent, and his hands on her breasts felt good.

"You *are* hungry this morning," she murmured, rising to her feet.

"I am. But I'm in no hurry. Take your time. Let's take our time." He paused. "How about something to eat?"

She couldn't quite tell from his tone if he was pulling back, responding to her strange declaration, or accepting it.

"Let me just throw some pants on." He went into the bathroom.

The breakfast buffet that greeted them was like a considerate old friend, offering something for her, something for him, *caccosa pe tutte,* something for everyone. Lisa chose fluffy scrambled red-yolk eggs and crisp little sausages like the ones she ate in the delicate croissant on Via Toledo. Ichiro chose a hard-boiled egg and salmon carpaccio and covered it with sour cream and chives. They both chose homemade yoghurt and fresh huckleberries—*mirtilli*—that still had dew clinging to their purple skin.

"Tutto bene?" The goggle-eyed desk clerk approached their table at the continental breakfast. *"Volete più caffè?"*

They smiled when he brought their refills. He asked them where they were from with none of the disapproval they'd sensed when they squished their way to his desk last night. Ichiro introduced them as "Lisa Greco, from New York," and "Ichiro Negroponte, from Tokyo."

The old man nodded. *"Lei canta be'*—You sing in Napoli," he said as though rumor of the Japanese tenor had made its way to Pozzuoli, "and last night at Campiglione."

"Thank you for recommending that place," Ichiro said.

"It was amazing," Lisa agreed. "We loved it."

"You have family here?"

"Long, long ago," Ichiro responded.

The old man nodded. "You have the same names."

The statement perplexed them, and their faces showed it.

"'Negroponte—Greco' the same," he expounded. "From *isole greche,* Euboea. Both 'false names.'" He looked at Lisa. "Your ancestors were called *Greco* because they were Greek," he tells her. "But that wasn't their real name. They were just called *Greco* by Etruscans who were here before them."

They looked at each other.

"Pozzuoli used to be famous as a resort," the man continued. "Virgil spent his holidays here to get away from the pressures of Rome. Saint Peter and Paul preached here, and it was here that San Gennaro was beheaded. It's where I was born and grew up." He paused.

"And your family name," he looked to Ichiro, "comes from the old name of the city of Chalkis, capital of Euboea." He took out his pen, and wrote words on the paper tablecloth. "The name is from the Greek phrase *στὸν Εὔριπον*, '*to Evripon*', corrupted into *στὸ Νεὔριπον* '*to Nevripon*', then in Campagna becoming 'Negroponte,' 'black bridge'—the *ponte*, 'bridge' being interpreted as the bridge that connected Chalkis with Attica."

"You mean three thousand years ago we might have been first cousins?" Lisa exclaimed.

That made Ichiro laugh.

"How do you know all this?" Lisa asked.

The old man turned his owl-like stare on her. "I was professor of Linguistic Etymology, at the University," he said. He bowed slightly. "*Mi chiamo Giose Rimanelli*." He shook her hand, then Ichiro's, who bowed in return. "*Euboea*," he continued. "Means 'good cow,' by the way. That's why I sent you to Campiglione." There was a slight trace of a smile on his lips.

But she saw the old professor was now staring at her pendant. An aged sadness filled his eyes.

"You wear *il fregio Greco*" ("the Greek frieze"), he finally said, appraising them both more carefully. "A wedding gift?"

"No," Lisa broke in. "A gift from a complete stranger."

"That indirectly led her here," Ichiro added.

Lisa was studying the old man. "Actually, the stranger looked like you, a little," she said. "He's the one who gave me the business card."

"I had a younger brother," Professor Rimanelli said. "He lived in Brooklyn. I haven't seen him for fifty years, since he left us for America." He seemed shaken.

"Thank you, *professore*," Ichiro said. "You've given us a lot to think about."

The old man didn't answer, just slowly walked away toward the kitchen. He turned back to look at them again. "Please don't leave yet. I will be back."

When he returned to the table, he pulled out a leather wallet that looked as old as he was. He reached into its change purse. Lisa saw a flash of gold as his hand came out.

In one gesture, he clasped Ichiro's hand in his and deposited what he'd taken from his wallet. "A wedding gift," he said. "A long time ago I was going to exchange it with my bride."

Ichiro frowned, and opened his hand.

It was a pendant.

Identical to hers.

"Why didn't you give it to her?" Lisa dared to ask.

The old man looked at her and she could see his eyes glimmered with tears. "She ran away to America. With my brother." His face was conflicted, as though wrestling with something. "We bought one for each of us," he finally said. "She had hers for me with her when she left with him."

Lisa's hands moved to take off the chain and hand it to him—but the old man shook his finger to stop her.

"But this is yours," she protested. "Let's say I brought it back for you. From your brother."

"I have no need of it now," he said. "You must keep them and let them together continue to guide you."

Lisa still felt dizzy. She felt like holding her head with both hands. Life was spinning.

"Serendipity is actually similar to the meander pattern," Ichiro was saying in a voice that showed the strain his mind, too, was experiencing. "But I prefer synchronicity, which recognizes structured purpose." Was he trying to distract her from the maelstrom within?

She thought she'd been on an unswerving path to finding out who she was, discovering her best self. Wasn't Ichiro one big swerve? She had to get her hands back on the wheel. Leaving her computers behind was giving her way too much time to think. Was this destiny's way of pulling the rug out from under her again?

They were passing through the Phlegraean Fields, with no green in sight. It's like the surface of the moon here, she observed with a chill, part of the caldera of a volcano that had once been every bit as active as Vesuvius a few miles to the east. Signs told them that this volcano had last erupted in 1538, and was considered still active. Great. Most of its crater, which measured eight miles across, was now underwater. The land was barren, a plateau strewn with rubble. Fire was bursting from the rocks in places, and clouds of sulfurous gas snaked out of vents that led deep underground.

She could see the hellish fields vanish into the sea now on their horizon. "What are you talking about?" she demanded. Her voice and his both sounded tinny and unreal, as if she were hearing them through a steel curtain, as though they were lost in a tunnel that deadened sound.

"The Unified Field Theory posits that all phenomena can be described in a single field. That the twisting of the DNA molecule resembles, topologically, the structure of the cosmos itself."

"Hunh?"

"So when life offers a link, for example one pendant to another, it can *not* be accidental. Einstein believed that life *had* to make sense. 'God does not play dice with the universe.' Synchronicity is what mathematics calls the 'unified field,' what non-mathematicians might call 'serendipity.'"

"But you can't really accept that the desk clerk and my dapper stranger are really brothers, can you? What are the odds?"

"That's simply the point," Ichiro said, the glint in his eye stronger than ever. "When all is known, and reduced to numerical equation, there *are* no odds. In retrospect, everything reveals intention."

Lisa was silent for a moment, trying to wrap her brain around how different his reaction was from hers. "Since, in reality, all is *not* known, what do we do with things like this?" She fingered her pendant.

"What do they do with us?"

She looked at him, baffled. "And the emotional solution to this conundrum?"

"It's entirely up to us. Our destiny, our solution, is what we decide it will be. We either embrace it or walk away. It's precisely that simple."

This time the pause was even longer before she responded. "Someone told me a long time ago that when you are approaching something and you become uncertain, stop approaching it until you are no longer uncomfortable."

"What's wrong with uncomfortable?" he asked.

She could hear the sincerity. He really meant it as a question.

And it was a good one.

Their day passed in a fog, details blurring together as they do in a lucid dream where you watch yourself walking toward the unknown like an automaton.

They reached the excavations at Baia. They passed the ruins of a temple and reached the narrow entrance to the cave leading to the Oracle of the Dead. "Notice the asymmetry," Ichiro said, "in contrast to the sibylline antrum."

"What do you make of that? Was it intentional?"

Ichiro nodded. "I think so. It was to distract the gods, who instilled in humans the love of symmetrical form. Maybe it was to hide something bigger than the gods, something more elemental."

Like Orpheus, Odysseus, and Aeneas before them, they slowly made their way along the narrow descending path, at each fork choosing the lower path. Who had built this maize of tunnels, and for what purpose? Why was the path less than two-feet wide? It moved for a few yards in one direction, then turned upon itself and moved in a different direction. Her claustrophobia was held in check only by Ichiro's presence. It reminded Lisa of the hairpin curves from a childhood camping trip to Colorado. Only here the view in both directions was solid stone. That made her shudder uncontrollably despite the heat.

"The S-bend construction is clearly meant to conceal direction and turn the mind inward, partially as an antidote to feeling overwhelmed by the unnatural environment."

"My zig-zags," Lisa whispered. She wanted to ask something. But she was numb, feeling nothing even when he took her hand. For a claustrophobic, what she was doing was unimaginable. She looked down on her progress into the earth as though from the ceiling of the passageway, as though she were someone else, a fantastical creature being led by a mysterious knight whose intentions were unfathomable. Was he using *her* as the key to some topological problem he was trying to solve? What could be so important to that girl in the tunnel that she would let herself be guided into her deepest fears? What was so important to the man that he would force her to face them with him?

She realized she was drenched with sweat. The temperature had been slowly increasing and she could see Ichiro had noticed it too. He offered her his handkerchief, and she accepted it gratefully and wiped away the perspiration that was dripping into her eyes and making them burn.

She smelled the water before she could hear it, and long before they saw it. He told her archaeologists who discovered this underground labyrinth in modern times called it "the River Styx, the last obstacle to cross before entering Hades."

When they turned the last S-bend and their angle of descent steepened even more, it wasn't the enveloping warm vapors smelling faintly of sulfur, or the warm water lapping onto the tunnel's pavement, that captured her attention.

It was what lay beneath the water, glistening with life even through the mist. As through a glass clearly.

The exact shape of their pendants multiplied many-fold, laid in ancient tile, covered by a foot or two of crystal-clear water.

Lisa sought his eyes. "Did you know this was here?" she asked.

Ichiro took her hands. "I did," he answered. "Discovering it was how I justified my coming to Naples, remember? When I began my research on Archimedes' question, I was told by a fellow topologist at the University in Naples that the ancient builders, probably Etruscans enslaved by the Greek newcomers, constructed it here as a template of the cosmos itself."

"What do you mean?" She caught her breath, feeling the dizziness again.

"Simply that it is the key to infinite *form*, the architectural schematic controlling all structure, from the galactic to the volcanic to the anthill."

"Explain."

"It contains within itself the power to expand infinitely, through as many iterations as the observer wishes to create. It's the ultimate evidence that a single line can fill any space available, including the entire universe. That is why it's sacred."

"What do *you* think?"

He was studying the tile carefully. "I think it is simply an elegant mathematical signal. A kind of universal map. Maybe even an antenna to broadcast or receive what we know about life."

She remembered the semiotics class she'd taken from Umberto Eco when he was visiting Yale from the University of Bologna. In semiotics, a signal was composed of sender, signal, and receiver. "Who is the sender? What does the signal mean? Who is the receiver?"

The appreciative look Ichiro gave her was not, she noted, the least bit patronizing. He respected her question without any element of condescension. "The meaning of the signal is 'infinity,'" he said. "It is a design created with pseudo-Hilbert curves that demonstrates how a single line can intersect every point in any chosen space from the smallest to the infinite."

"And the sender?"

"The past," he shrugged. "The accumulated wisdom of all who have lived and thought before us."

"And we are the receivers?"

He nodded. "Yes, the present. Ours, and all those in the future."

She touched her pendant, and the touch electrified her. In the strangest of ways, it had served as a map for her too. Nothing like ordinary maps that showed you the lines that connected there and here. It was a map of indirection, a wanderer's map, a meander map that allowed her freedom of decision and at one and the same time brought her to where she was meant to be. And certainly it was also a signal.

She reached out for Ichiro's arm to steady herself, the claustrophobia falling on her unexpected as though it had lurked around this very corner for eternity in expectation of her as its sacrificial victim.

"Kiss me." He pulled her to him.

"If I kiss you now, I may lose myself forever," she said, not understanding the meaning of her own words.

But the kiss was unavoidable.

There was nothing tentative about it.

Their lips came together, their tongues, with a primitive heat that warmed this cold chamber and insulated them from harsh stone and impassive tile. This was the kiss worth waiting for, a kiss worth a journey across the face of the earth—a once-in-a-lifetime kiss that could never be described or repeated. And she let herself fall into it, until her identity separated from the essence of this doubling they created and disappeared into the dark stillness of the deepest meditation she'd ever experienced.

But it wasn't her experiencing it.

It was they, together as though they were one.

She had no idea how long it lasted—seconds, minutes, hours? There was no way to measure this intensity.

A bright light swept away the deep-down dark into which they had plunged; and suddenly, in the heart of their abyss, she was facing her fear as though in a mirror.

And the fear was pulling her back to the surface.

"Whoa," Ichiro was saying. "I'm losing you."

Twenty-three

THE JIGSAW PUZZLE THEY'D BEEN constructing together flew apart on the drive back. At first they drove in silence, both reeling from what they had felt together in the cave. But what came next for Lisa was full retreat.

Retreat to a safe distance.

She needed to get her bearings. She needed to figure out the trajectory of her life, *on her own,* without the convenient coincidence of this pairing she'd happened on by accident.

Yet, no matter what tempest was crashing around inside her, Ichiro remained cool.

Too cool for me, she concluded. Face him with the gnarliest dilemma and his mind turns to logic and analysis with no interference from emotion. How could this possibly end up? Her American spark and his Japanese *sangfroid.* It wasn't what she needed right now. The guilt she'd been holding in abeyance was now upon her in full force. She had turned her back on the very reason she came to Italy. Would her work still be waiting for her when she returned to Fabio's?

Leaving her laptop *and* cell phone behind was a terrible decision. They were her anchors to the world she created by herself. She couldn't even believe she'd done it.

An even darker thought had announced itself. Would they even be there? Might they have been stolen, in this city notorious for its thieves? Or held hostage by Fabio, in revenge for her abandonment of him at the ball?

Her free-wheeling wandering into fantasy had even made her lose track of the calendar. Wasn't *today* the last day she'd booked through Airbnb? Was Fabio expecting her to vacate the breathtakingly inspiring premises in the morning?

She stared at Ichiro. He still appeared oblivious to her racing mind, his eyes coolly focused on the road ahead.

He was light with clarity.

She was heavy with confusion.

On the drive to Baia, they'd talked about gods and heroes descending to the underground. She remembered the one-hour therapist telling her that "we have to descend into the unconscious before we can make conscious sense of our lives." She told Ichiro that.

"The pattern of the surface is revealed *below* the surface," he said. "The underlying formula determines whether a trajectory is forward or backward or spinning random."

"But random is what got us here, what brought us together?" she'd half-asked, half-stated.

"I was getting to that." He gave her a piercing look. "I told you I don't believe in random. As long as human nature remains what it is, it simply makes no sense."

She'd fallen silent. Her life was flipping before her eyes like a Power-Point presentation gone amok. She had been on such an orderly progression—from high school graduate, to Yale prodigy, to "preferred hire" at Standard, to designated successor to her prodigious boss—and she'd thrown it all away. She'd let herself go from being a tightly-woven, productive, successful professional to an irresponsibly liberated, creatively headstrong, impetuous human being—egged on by the most incongruous clown-egghead she could have imagined. It was an unsustainable lark.

Her experience when they found the meander tiles in the depths of the cave frightened her most. She'd made a monumental mistake leaping into the unknown. Until her unguarded chemistry with this easy-living matho-musician exploded, she had been taking careful, and progressively positive, steps. She'd broken out of Manhattan, made it back to the land of her dreams, centered herself, and discovered a tangible, promising relationship with her real work in life—with her writing.

So deluded had she let herself become that she was actually readying herself to make the jump from one perfectly enviable life to the unknown country of creativity.

She wasn't thinking straight. She'd fallen under the spell of a Pied Piper.

This lark was a confusing detour.

Her weakness for magic had led her to allow herself this emotional excursion, which now jeopardized everything she'd worked toward.

They had to return the Acura with a full tank, so Ichiro pulled off into an Ofanto Sud. "We can get an espresso at the same time," he said.

She went in with him and stood at the crowded stainless steel coffee bar and tried to find something to say. But he didn't give her the chance.

"I know I don't have the perfect tan like your landlord, and a swimming pool of my own among my vast properties."

She tried to laugh, thinking he was teasing, but it quickly turned to anger when she realized he wasn't.

"Please tell me you're joking," she said. "I'm not the least bit interested in my playboy landlord. He invited me. I'd never been to a masked ball before, so I accepted it for the experience."

"Like you accepted my invitation to Cumae?" He spoke like he was weighing every word.

Were the other travelers looking at them? She couldn't be sure. She lowered her voice a little. "That was *my* idea. Or don't you remember?" She paused, took a breath. "What's going on here?"

He took a breath as well, bowing his head slightly. "What is going on is that I'm losing you. You are going away. You are turning your back."

"Turning my back on what?" she demanded.

"On the future of the trajectory we were assigned to," he finally said.

The man closest to them had finished his coffee, but paused to listen.

"And what trajectory is that exactly? How long can you sustain this metaphor?" Lisa was irritated that he had jumped to conclusions faster than she could reach them.

"We were tracing the origins of our individual lines. We discovered they converged in a labyrinth that we could happily explore without limitation." His voice trailed off, as though the effort to communicate was futile. "Then you succumbed to your claustrophobia—and ran."

It's true. She had. Literally. She ran at full tilt up the narrow tunnels, gasping for air. Desperate to be free from the chill stone walls that had suddenly felt like a suffocating blanket—and not a comforting one at all.

"I needed to breathe," she said, when he caught up with her at the asymmetrical entrance to the shaft.

"I understand," Ichiro said.

The listener left, giving them an ambivalent look, as though he wished he could stay for the end.

"This wasn't supposed to be two days." She wasn't sure what she was trying to explain. "I guess I'm feeling guilty for taking two days off."

The truth was that Lisa was experiencing "pre-rejection jitters," known only to writers—the absolute conviction that the work she'd submitted to Kevin would be met with ridicule and destroy any credibility she'd been painstakingly building up for years. That she'd slammed one door shut before another one had even presented itself.

But how could she admit that? She was having enough trouble with the feeling itself, irrational or not, without subjecting herself to Ichiro's kind of cool-headed analysis.

Ichiro grinned at her. "Think about it. These days counted. You simply can't take days off from your own life."

She kissed him on the cheek. "I've loved exploring with you. It's been thrilling. And I know there's much more that could be discovered. But I'm simply not at a point in my life that I can go on with it right now. I need to go back and sort things out first."

"Haven't you been sorting all your life?" he asked.

"Sort of," she retorted.

"And how was that working out for you?"

"You've watched too much American television," she scolded, then grew serious again: "I think it *was* working out, just that it hadn't been clear enough to me until now *what* was working out, what I wanted. Doesn't that make sense? I can find a balance, as you have, without throwing one part of me away."

"What makes sense isn't always the right path. The jumps beyond sense are what lead to the greatest discoveries. If you let life take care of you, if you trust it, you'll be surprised how well things might work out. If you decide with your heart instead of over-worked brain you might find what you're looking for."

"Look who's taking! How do you know what I'm looking for?"

"I see it in your eyes."

She took his hand, pressed it into both of hers. "Ichiro, meeting you was one of the great highlights of my life. I won't lose sight of that, I promise you. I just need time."

He bowed to her, formally and solemnly—and with an air of poignant finality. "Then take your time," he said but not without adding: "It is only yours for the taking."

Did she detect a tiny twinkle in his eye? She wasn't sure. And, for once, she left it at that. She didn't need the last word.

As she closed the green door, she imagined she heard him walking away:

> *La donna è mobile*
> *Qual piuma al vento,*
> *Muta d'accento — e di pensier.*

> The lady is fickle
> Like a feather in the wind,
> She changes her tone, like her mind.

Twenty-four

BY THE TIME SHE GOT back to the flat, Fabio wasn't around. Instead he'd left a note attached to her door: "Please vacate by eleven tomorrow. *Grazie*. Fabio." Short, but not sweet. In a strange way, she was relieved. Time to reenter reality again, take back control. Sort her own life out.

She let herself in, and ran immediately to the bedroom. Her phone and laptop were still intact.

Both needed charging.

But the minute they were plugged in, the machines that pulled her strings began to spew out their missives to her.

She could barely sleep, so much did the mechanical message monsters wind her up. She finally collapsed, without undressing, around three—only to awaken from wind-tossed dreams to go back to her sorting.

Kevin demanded that she return. Honor your commitments, "keep your present reservations." That "it's the right way to do it." Do what? She wondered.

Elation, trepidation, fear, giddiness, disbelief flooded her mind and heart as one by one she tried to discern the pattern, like a detective assembling scattered clues—until she saw the emails fitting together to form the new puzzle of her life:

Phyllis' anger at her request for time reversed overnight when Larry Thompson let it be known that he "would be ankling"—would not honor the contract—without Standard's promise that Lisa, and only Lisa, would be his editor. Who used the word "ankling" in New York? Larry's been reading *Hollywood Reporter* too long.

But then Larry finished her manuscript.

Sent it to Kevin.

Kevin read it.

They talked.

They sent it to Phyllis, demanding that she read it.

She read it. Flipped for it. "Make her an offer she can't refuse"—this from Kevin, who made the offer:

"$125,000, 1/3 on signing, 1/3 on delivery, 1/3 on publication; with an option on the next novel at the same rate."

From Phyllis: "We are working out your termination agreement, waiting here for your signature. It will include your promise to continue editing Thompson, billing us by the hour, from wherever you are as long as he desires it. Plus an exit package of $125,000 payable upon signing, and also retain full benefits as long as your books remain with Standard."

Her mind was reeling as she continued the sorting:

Kevin would be throwing a party at Michael's for her this coming weekend. "Jet-lagged or not, you need to be there."

"Oh, yeah," his next email began. "You need to resign formally, so your termination package can commence—and we aren't stuck with unemployment compensation issues."

That made her snort.

Finally, from Larry Thompson, offering to edit her book if she'd like—and, "of course," to endorse it.

Her train was at three, return flight at six-thirty. She half-thought of ignoring the emails, and just arriving at Standard Friday morning to deal with it all. Instead, she wrote just to Larry, thanking him for his intervention, and to Kevin, telling him what time her flight arrived. Then she threw her things into her suitcase, realizing how different they looked from the black and gray array that had arrived with her.

She'd skipped breakfast, so she pulled on her Desigual jeans and the bright red halter top and ran across Via Toledo to grab something at the nearest restaurant. She found *Il Cucciolo* in Vico Berio, the first alley to the left of the largo Augusteo.

It was early, and she was the first customer. So what else is new? The elderly waiter was still tying on his white apron. As he carefully maneuvered the four marble steps separating the dining room from the foyer, she realized he must be in his eighties. A fall might change his life forever. He looked as though he had no fears in the world other than not being able to show up for a job he'd enjoyed for maybe three-quarters of a century. Her heart soared. He didn't *need* to work. He *loved* to work. He revered his work.

That was Napoli.

That was her.

She thought about all the wonderful meals she'd enjoyed in her weeks here and couldn't make up her mind at first. By the time the waiter had served her mineral water and quarter-carafe of red wine, she came to a decision:

"*Sulo un piatto di pummarole, Signor, pe ppiace*" ("Just a plate of tomatoes, please") she told him. "*Senza muzzarella*" ("without mozzarella"), she added. She'd seen the tomatoes laid out near the door as

161

she entered and they were exactly what she felt like: something simple.

As she relished the ripe tomatoes, she heard the voice of reality reinforcing her decision. She must go back, deal with things professionally. Then she could, if she wanted, return with a clear mind.

The old waiter merely beamed at her and brought her the plate of tomatoes, adorned with a few sprigs of fresh basil for color. They were so red and bright—and sweet—that she rejoiced: She'd imagined exactly what she wanted, and received from the *abbondanza* of this miraculous siren city exactly what she'd imagined.

Filled with regrets and flavors left behind, her bullet train for Fiumicino departed precisely at three, rolling quietly from Napoli Centrale north to its rendezvous with Rome. Its sleek gray and red flanks, newly washed, reflected the station's pillars one by one, slower then faster, as it gained the momentum to leave Parthenope behind.

But Lisa Greco was not aboard.

She'd followed her logic and proceeded to the train station. She'd watched her train roll in from Messina. But her feet had refused when she directed them to board. It felt all wrong. She stood rooted, overwhelmed by a new sense of loss, one she couldn't remember ever feeling. It wasn't the fear of losing herself. It was fear of something even worse, something bigger than herself, more important. If she left, who knows where life might take her? Was she really prepared to navigate a trajectory that moved toward the past she'd left behind, and away from the past she'd just begun to experience? Was she really prepared to risk never coming back to this city of enchantment that had welcomed her with open arms?

So she watched the train depart, watched until it receded into the distance and left only empty track—trajectory not taken—with tears leaking from her eyes that made no sense at all.

She sat on a bench on the platform and tried to meditate. But her eyes refused to close and her thoughts refused to go away. She had descended into a claustrophobic's nightmare and, after all, nothing had happened. Except that she had faced fear. Was that such a bad thing? If she could do that and survive, could she not do anything? Suddenly she remembered the word that described the exact feeling she had that first rainy morning in Napoli. The word was Finnish: *kaukokaipuu*, "homesickness felt for a place one has never been." She'd registered the odd word strongly when she ran across it in yet another book she'd proposed only for Standard to turn down: *The Book of Human Emotions* by Tiffany Watt Smith. The marketing department had practically said, "no one cares," though Little, Brown a few months later did pretty well with it. She remembered the word not only because it was precise, but also because it book-ended the feeling she'd called pre-nostalgia, which she experienced whenever she'd thought about going to Italy. She felt that going there and coming back would fill her with a nostalgia so intense she might never survive it. That led her to surely the wildest thought she'd ever had. What if she never went back? Lisa tried to slam the green door in her brain shut against that thought but it wasn't easy, and the door would not fully shut.

Last night she'd made a firm decision that it was her destiny telling her to go home and square things away, as Kevin urged. Sure, she'd fantasized about exploring life here in Naples with Ichiro, but she forced herself to admit she could not see its shape; she had no map. Until she stood at the actual door to the coach, she had day-dreamed that Ichiro, bearing a bouquet of operatic roses, would show up to stop her. That they'd kiss on the platform as the train rolled away, and then walk into the sunset together. All it takes for a clear mind is for you to clear it, Ichiro had said.

Now, when that had not happened, she tried again to take a deep breath, close her eyes, and meditate. But her mind was filled with tumbling images of sun, blue sky, darker blue sea—of *alici* and *vongole*, of street singers and dancing teenagers, of the view of St. Elmo from Rossini's flat. She gently nudged the images aside with her mantra. But they kept coming back.

This city just plain wasn't finished with her yet.

Even in the depths of her meditation, she could hear the fast footsteps of someone running from the direction of the station entrance. At first her mantra battled with the insistent sound, but as the sound approached, the mantra stilled itself, quieted by the certainty growing in her heart.

The familiar voice intruded, singing the familiar song. Was it inside her, or not? Another tear fell from her tightly closed eyes. She didn't dare open them. She didn't want to know for sure. But the running footsteps had stopped and the song continued.

Che bella cosa 'na jurnata 'e sole
  How beautiful is a sunny day
N'aria serene doppo 'na tempesta
  The air serene after the storm
Pe'll'aria fresca pare già 'na festa
  The fresh air is a celebration
Che bella cosa 'na jurnata e'sole
  What a beautiful thing, a sunny day.

She felt something in her hand, and opened her eyes. It was a single red rose. She held it to her nose as he sang:

> *Ma n'atu sole*
>> *But there's another sun*
>
> *Cchiu' bello oi ne'*
>> *That's more beautiful*
>
> *'O sole mio*
>> *It's my sun—*
>
> *Sta 'nfronte a te*
>> *Your face*
>
> *'O sole 'O sole mio*
>> *My sun—my only sun*
>
> *Sta 'nfronte a te*
>> *It's your face*
>
> *Sta 'nfronte a te*
>> *It's your face*

She saw that his eyes, too, were shining with tears. "You're a little late, aren't you?"

"I had to find the right rose," he said, taking her in his arms.

Epilogue

WHEN LISA NEXT LOOKED AT her phone, she saw a text from Larry: He was hopping a plane for Italy, would spend a few days in Rome with old friends, then come to Naples when she told him that she finished her manuscript so they could celebrate and discuss both their books.

Ichiro protected her morning work sessions and bought them more time together by rescheduling his voice classes at the University. He'd moved out of his cell-like room at Casa Napoli on Spaccanapoli to a small suite the two of them now shared, with a stunning view of the city spilling down from Vesuvius. "Life in the shadow of death," Lisa described it.

"Of course," Ichiro said. "That is how the labyrinth is defined—the preconditioning suppositions that—"

She interrupted him with a kiss. He loved that. He would remove her red glasses—he said the black ones made her look like a librarian—and held her cheeks in his hands as the kiss continued.

Casa Napoli was owned by Donna Isolata, who soon became Lisa's best friend and confidant, signing her up for a class in Neapolitan taught by an elegant young woman who showed up for the first class in a skin-tight turquoise suede suit that gave Lisa a whole new take on style. It was Donna Isolata who taught her how to make pizza Quattro Stagione—a quarter of each pizza devoted to each of the four seasons: *pummadore* and *basilico* for summer; *funghi selvaggi* (wild mushrooms), for fall; white *fiori di latte* cheese and carpaccio for winter; and *carciofi* (artichokes), for spring. Donna Isolata insisted she sprinkle grated fresh garlic on all four quarters to keep Ichiro's voice in tune.

It was after one of his nights knocking 'em dead at A' Canzuncella that Ichiro led her to the Fontana della Sirena, just beyond the Riviera di Chiaia on Viale Antonio Gramschi. The beauty of the marble fountain, illuminated by floods that made rainbows of the water, took her breath away. But she preferred the other siren fountain, the one carved into the side of Santa Caterina della Spinacorona that showed Parthenope looking like a winged angel with feathered legs. Surely the sculptor was enshrining the irrepressible humor of this city. Ichiro called it *Fontana delle Zizze*, "fountain of the breasts," because the spouting waters were issuing from angelic Parthenope's breasts—dousing the flames of Vesuvius. *Dum Vesevi Syrena Incendia Mulcet* (While the Mermaid softens the fire of Vesuvius) was carved into the marble.

Their lovemaking, when it happened, happened spontaneously after their *passegiatta* the entire length of Spaccanapoli, the ancient straight line that led from Piazza Gesù Nuovo to the Palazzo di Monte Pietà in the hills of the Quartieri Spagnoli. As they walked arm in arm, Lisa observed that couples chatted constantly—"until they marry. Will we keep chatting?" she asked.

"We'll simply have to experiment," he said, with a wink of light in his eyes.

Then she spotted what she was looking for, a tiny shop marked *Gioielli antichi,* antique jewelry. "Wait here," she ordered Ichiro.

He looked puzzled, but complied.

When she came out of the shop, she asked, "Where is your Greek key?"

Ichiro produced it from his pocket. She opened her fist to reveal the antique gold chain, and deftly slipped his key onto it. His eyes widened as she slipped the chain and pendant over his head. He started to kiss her. "Grazie," he said. "*M'aspettà,* but wait." He lifted the chain from his neck and placed it over her head, then took hers for his. They kissed, like Neapolitans, in full view of everyone on the street. Who smiled in approval as the kiss went on, and on.

Though there was giggling and deep breathing, no words were said when they returned to Casa Napoli. They fell into each other's arms, their mouths came together and, with a flow that seemed choreographed by life itself, found themselves naked and in bed. She rejoiced to feel his light and clarity enter into the darkness of her labyrinth and fill her soul with light and joy.

The dark shadows of her past were dissipating. With Ichiro, and her work, and the rearrangements with Standard, Lisa Greco was walking toward that light. "When you walk toward light, with every step," she wrote, "all gets brighter and brighter."

THE END

Know that all of Nature is but a magic theater,
That the great Mother is the master magician,
And that this whole world is peopled by her many parts.

—Upanishads [from David Lynch's *Catching the Big Fish*]

To the Reader

Thank you for reading my story. I truly appreciate your time. We writers write to be read, and without you there *is* no point in writing. I'd be most appreciative if you'd take a moment to review this novella. Reviewers are important to a writer's visibility! And I'd love to hear from you directly, with suggestions for future romances—or otherwise: andreaaguillard@storymerchant.com.

THE CIRCLING STONES OF ALLISON REID

One

HER HEIGHT WAS THE SCOURGE of her existence, a handicap she woke up with every morning and took to bed with her each night. From the age of twelve, Allison Reid grew to tower over her classmates, one by one. By fourteen, there was no one in first year high school who didn't, literally, look up to her. What skirts were for other girls were miniskirts for her. Their jeans were her capris. Tights were a particular bane.

Her own personal race for the moon finally ended when she reached six-foot-three in her junior year at UCLA and a random fellow undergrad would cross the campus to tell her, "God, you're tall!" She would give him a withering look and he would back away, still staring at her—and often while attempting a selfie—as though he'd snuck a peek into a carnival show.

And she would feel like that freak, and it gave her the creeps.

She watched other tall girls slouch to the level of their friends, especially boyfriends, and decided she wasn't ever going to do that. It made her angry. Their slouches would become permanent. She would stand up straight and carry herself as proudly as a princess.

She loved wearing heels but guys got weird when she did. So she stopped pursuing boys when she was still in her late teens. If they pursued her, and she sparked to them, she just might give it a shot. Or she might just wear higher heels and let them go their way.

She'd never get lost in a crowd.

Top shelf requests, ceiling fans, subway trains, giraffe jokes, "How's the weather up there?" and Smart Cars—these were the slings and arrows of her outrageous fortune.

And don't get her started on weight. An average woman's fat weight was Allison's skinny weight. Few men she'd encountered were going to whisk her into their arms and carry her over a threshold, at least not without serious lumbar risk. And, no, she wasn't kicking the back of that airline seat in front of her; her knees were simply lock-jammed into a space designed for another species or another era.

Over time, Allison got off on being taller. It gave her perspective. And it was an unfailing test of a male's self-confidence. If he couldn't handle her, he wasn't worth her time. You'd think men would be attracted to women like her, but she soon learned the words "tall sip of water" and "Amazonian" weren't exactly compliments. Most men she'd been interested in initially were soon intimidated, if not downright emasculated once they got within chatting distance. They were looking for the girl next door—five-foot-four, eyes of blue, goochie, goochie, goo—not the girl two stories up that they needed a stepladder to kiss.

When she encountered other tall women in crowds, they formed an immediate rapport. Or at least a respectful exchange of smiles on the elevator, one veteran acknowledging another. Tall women looked out for each other. Literally.

◎

Being tall wasn't her only distinction. Allison Reid was also first in her class. In everything. She saw other smart girls, cerebral slouchers, miss questions on purpose to avoid the embarrassment of "standing out." She *already* stood out so she'd be damned not to do her very best in all things: math and English, gym and music, geography and world affairs, psychology—especially psychology.

That she also happened to be a natural blonde compounded the curse. Tall, blonde, and smart. Yikes. The perfect storm. And certainly not what most men were looking for. Most of the guys she encountered at mixers and athletic events simply chose not to accept the reality that was her. Their idea of a cool pickup line was the dumb blonde joke.

Question: "Which one is farther away, the moon or Houston?"
Dumb blonde: "Duh. Houston! You can *see* the moon!"
Give me a break.

She learned earlier than normal-sized girls that happiness need come from within because she clearly understood that the odds of finding that "tall, dark, and handsome" prince to set all things right were not at all in her favor. She figured if such fairy tales were to come true, the guy would hunt her down when the time came.

Besides, why couldn't she handle life on her own? She didn't need a man to do that.

So prince charming hadn't shown up, and she was now thirty-three. But she was happy. She'd done well enough for herself, by herself. She'd taken night classes and received her master's in Sociology & Psychology. Now, thanks to the UCLA Placement office, she had a solid job as a civil servant—with the side benefit of being nearly unfireable.

Although it was strictly nine to five and a bit constricting, the job was satisfying. She gave divorced women a leg up in getting their lives back on track. Most of the time they'd curtailed their education to serve their men who'd now achieved the success they'd dreamed of together—and promptly threw them over for a younger model. Allison lived for getting that phone call from one of her clients reporting she'd just received her B.A. from Marymount, or just been hired in a sweet position at Santa Monica City Hall, or just started her own garden design company.

Instead of heading down to celebrate at the local bar with her girlfriends where she'd be doomed to fend off lame tall blonde jokes, she'd learned to stay at home with or without a friend. Preferably near the fireplace, stocking feet on the coffee table, glass of champagne in hand—toasting the sweet triumph of seeing a sister take a giant step forward to self-fulfillment. In moments like this, she was proud of herself. Proud of figuring things out. Proud of doing it all on her own. It was enormously satisfying.

Then came the presidential election, and the Republican victory, clouded with electoral doubt, of an eccentric conservative with dubious intelligence. Whose minions were now, among other things, eyeing her department for annihilation. "Why is it necessary to give divorced women counseling at the tax payer's expense? If they aren't smart enough to stay married, why should that be our problem?"

Fuck them!

She for one could think of dozens of responses to that—and not all of them were self-serving. But politics made her so furious these days she forced herself to think of something else. She'd learned long ago that you can't change people who see no need to be changed, and she was not going to waste her precious time trying.

Her job was to show up at her office each morning bright and early and to throw her heart into serving her new clients. Like May Drexler, who'd been married to Los Angeles Times reporter Clay Drexler for twenty years and stalwartly raised their two sons until a red-headed journalism intern took him out for a beer one night two months ago and Clay had the brilliant epiphany that the intern was the woman he was meant for.

Allison was the first to reassure May that her experience had nothing to do with her self-confessed shortcomings and everything to do with the behavior of the twenty-first-century American male. "Why don't you try looking the other way until his fling burns itself out?" she suggested at first.

But May wasn't having it. "I never really loved him," she shrugged. "We were married too young and the twins came along before we could start thinking straight again. This hottie gives me my ticket to ride. If I don't do this now, I'll be unhappy the rest of my life."

Allison admired her grit and dug into her bag of tricks to inventory May's assets and liabilities so she could help her build a bridge to a future she could fall in love with.

When her two-week vacation came due, Allison was on the verge of letting it accrue, adding to her current accumulation of several months, when May happened to mention at lunch after one of her sessions that she was determined to visit London for the first time. "I've dreamed about it all my life," she said. "I was an English major at Occidental and want to see where Chaucer started his pilgrimage, where Dr. Johnson wrote his dictionary, where Shakespeare staged his plays. I owe it to myself," she argued, "and besides the bastard bought me an open-ended round-trip ticket after one of his most flagrant over-night absences. I'll be damned if I don't use it before I launch into real estate classes." Then she stared directly at Allison. "Why don't you come with me?"

The truth was, Allison had always been curious about London, and about England in general. She was British on both sides—her mother's family from Canterbury, her father's from a mysterious county known either as Cumbria or Cumberland, he wasn't sure which—but neither showed much interest in their land of origins or much patience with young Meggie's curious questions. Margaret was her middle name, her maternal grandmother's name; her mother nicknamed her Meggie, a name she couldn't wait to grow out of. Her father called her Al.

The parental units were too busy, never seeming to catch up with themselves since the advent of email. When texting came along, they became hopeless and more and more distant until their deaths in a freeway accident two years ago when they achieved ultimate distance from their only child.

But not before leaving Allison an insurance nest egg that her mother referred to as "mad money." She hadn't yet touched it because she hadn't needed to.

"I really can't." The words rolled out as though from a taped announcement. She decided it was a conflict of interest to be vacationing with a client. "But you have a wonderful time. I expect selfies on a daily basis."

May giggled.

She was so ready for this adventure, Allison thought. "We'll resume when you're back. Enjoy every minute. Bon voyage."

To Be Continued

ACKNOWLEDGMENTS

Without editors, a book can't be a book. I'm profusely grateful to have the team of Chi-Li Wong, Lisa Cerasoli, Chelsea Mongird, Danielle Canfield—and Kenneth Atchity—at my back. Thank you.

THE MEANDER TILE OF
LISA
GRECO